THE DARK
SIDE OF MAN

THE DARK
SIDE OF MAN

Franklin Lafayette King

*t*P
Texture Press
2015

Published in the United States by
Texture Press
1108 Westbrooke Terrace
Norman, OK 73072

For ordering information,
visit the Texture Press website at
www.texturepress.org

ISBN-13: 978-0-692-39578-3
ISBN-10: 0-692-39578-4

Cover painting by Franklin L. King

Book design by Arlene Ang

PREFACE

In the 1650s approximately 50,000 Irish slaves were sent to Barbados to work in the sugarcane fields of the island. None of these slaves were ever to return to Ireland. From the turmoil of slavery, the advent of piracy and the wars between the English, French and Dutch, the dark side of man emerged. I am the direct descendant of either a master or slave who lived in Barbados during this tumultuous page of human history.

The past transforms us all by forces unseen, perhaps to be revealed later in a dream.

—FLK

THE DARK SIDE OF MAN

I held you and love did smile within my sight.
Tropic nights when warm seas embraced the sandy beach.
The moon a disk of pagan light.

Your touch the crest of my desire
Wine, mirth and song upon the night.
A dove too soon calling us to awake in the fiery dawn.

It was not my desire that love should flee.
The hours of success did march by you and me.
Faults paraded in pomp and pageantry.

Now only the twilight of love remains.
Nights of repetition; longings unfulfilled.
A touch desired yet denied by both you and me.

Ocean swells crash upon the rock-strewn shore below.
The top of clouds hidden, where sun does cast its brilliant light,
Warm waters of the Caribbean Sea flow past
unseen in the silent night.

It is within us all revealed,
The searching heart fulfilled in vagrant love.
The dark side of man now seen.

TABLE OF CONTENTS

CHAPTER ONE
Barbados, 1651

FINN O'FLAHERTY FELT THE THUD of the hard wooden deck of the English ship. Many cuts and bruises tarnished his youthful complexion. The beauty of his bright brown eyes was now clouded by the colors of fatigue. Once imposing in a crowd of friends, he was thin and bent. He had been cast aboard the vessel like a sailor tosses a sea bag, his hands and feet still bound with rough hemp rope.

Finn was a muscular young man of 18, his black hair long and unkempt. His face had grown thin revealing well-defined features sculptured by hardships during the recent conflict between the English of Cromwell, the loyalists and the native Irish. His eyes were a deep brown that no longer sparkled with an uncommon clarity. Alongside him was Odhran O'Dea, the taller of the two. Like Finn, he stood over six feet tall in his bare feet. Their uncommon heights made them both stand out from the others.

Like Finn, Odhran's skin was sunburned from the long hours in which he had been exposed to the rain and cold of the rolling hills of Ireland. Both lads had been captured in the Siege of Drogheda, a battle fought on the east coast of Ireland. The Irish resistance to the harsh rule under Sir Oliver Cromwell's command had been handed a near fatal blow in the siege in which no mercy had been granted once the Irish commander had refused the English terms of surrender. The city's defenders had resisted valiantly to no avail as the guns of the English continued to slaughter the inhabitants until the blood of men, women and children sought the Irish Sea.

Earlier in the morning, Finn and Odhran had been herded to the stone quay at Inishbofin, a rocky now treeless island off the Connemara coast in Western Ireland. The "Island of the White Cow" had become a staging area for Cromwell's troops and a point of departure for various campaigns against the British loyalist and the Irish. The nearby stone barracks looked more like a monastery than a prison in the twilight of the morning. In the distance a corncrake's call could be heard among the screams of the seagulls and storm petrels. The soggy clothes of the two prisoners weighed heavily upon their thin bodies.

Two weeks earlier, Finn and Odhran had been marched across Ireland along with six fellow prisoners. The other men had been hung for attempting to escape; only Finn and Odhran have been spared. The two Irishmen were both young and stout, just what the English plantation owners needed in the distant island of Barbados.

"Odhran, where are they taking us?" asked Finn as he struggled to raise himself above the railing of the ship.

"I don't know. To hell, I suppose," replied Odhran. Still bound securely, he too struggled to his knees. Deep within the hull, they could hear a strange, melodic language being spoken.

"Odhran, this must be slaver. There are Africans locked in the hole. We are on a vessel bound to purgatory!"

They could feel the rocking movement of the ship as she lay alongside the quay. Their bindings had made their skin tender and sore, their feet shoeless on the wet cold deck. The sky above them was cloudy with a steady rain falling from the dark clouds that raced above the island towards the Connemara coast of Western Ireland.

"Slack the lines fore and aft! Slack the spring lines! Cast off all lines!" shouted the English Captain, his skin scarred by the sun; his eyes deeply recessed beneath his thick graying hair. The epaulettes of his rank hung heavily upon his shoulders, his woolen coat provided little protection from the soaking it now received in the downpour that fell upon the decks of the man-of-war.

The vessel slowly drifted away from the quay as two small vessels pulled the ship into the narrow channel, keeping her heading steady between the two spits of land.

Sailors had earlier scurried up the ratlines as the ship's drum beat the order to get underway. The tide had risen just enough for the deep-draft man-of-war to clear the rocks that lay submerged beneath the shallow entrance to the harbor. The crew loosened the sails secured about the spars of the frigate commissioned as the HMS *Wales*. She responded quickly to her freedom and drove her prow into the Atlantic, green salt water cascading upon the decks. Her bow-harvesting flying fish like a farmer's plow.

The HMS *Wales* was a ship of the line, a superb example of an English ship built from Irish wood, designed for the speed necessary in the pursuit of French vessels. Her brightly polished brass binnacle sparkled in the spray-filled wind. Soon she was cleanly cutting through the swells.

"Come to course 195!" shouted the first mate.

"Coming to course 195," responded the helmsman. "Steering course 195!"

Finn looked at Odhran. "Course 195. That means that we are heading southwest. There is nothing south of us except the end of the earth. Why are we aboard a warship with African slaves? Nothing makes sense."

"With a southwesterly course, we must be heading towards the islands of the western sea. This isn't a slaver but a ship of the line and a fine one, too. She is probably headed to the Caribbean to engage the French. First they will drop the slaves off and then go to quarters. What I don't understand is why we are aboard," said Finn as the salt spray stung his eyes. They were left bound on the deck since all hands had been quickly needed to lower the clouds of sail from the spars above them. The sails and lines quickly became taut in the strong wind.

THE TWO PRISONERS HAD EARLIER WATCHED their fellow Irishmen go to their deaths one by one in the late evening twilight of a day that could not be forgotten, their voices now filled Finn's dream.

"Sir Longford, I want to make an example of those seven men who attempted to escape. Take them to the summit of Benbulbin and have them hanged," Cromwell's lieutenant said loudly so the bound men could hear his command.

"My lord, why the summit?" Sir Philip Longford questioned. "It is a treacherous mountain even in the warmest of months."

"You have two prisoners that did not attempt to escape. Have them help the condemned men carry the scaffolding to the top. There is little wood left in Ireland to hang a man with and certainly no trees on top of that godforsaken mountain. I desire that you leave four men to watch over their bodies until the petrels have stripped the flesh from them. I want to make sure that no Irishman tries to take them down until the word has spread throughout Donegal."

"My lord, the summit is many meters high. No one will be able to see them hanging there."

"Sir Longford, I don't give a damn if any Irishman sees them. I want the word to spread in the streets and pubs. I want them to see the bodies in their minds. Then they will understand how futile it is to resist Cromwell's reach. After they are hanged, I want fifty men dispatched to every village to announce what we have done. Tell the people that their sacred mountain wears the bodies of their kin."

Sir Longford paused, then with hesitation said, "I am not certain, my lord, that we have enough wood to hang them with."

"Take a detail to their churches and pull the wood from their walls and altars." Sir Godfrey smiled. "Tell the bastards that they will be hung on consecrated wood. That should comfort them."

Finn and Odhran stood among the condemned. They now realized the conditions under which the hangings were to occur and for what purpose they were to serve. The condemned also knew that they would carry their own scaffolding aided by only two boys.

The next day, a small group of men under Sir Longford returned with a wagon loaded with beams sufficient for the task of hanging the condemned. Several local churches had been stripped of their fine wood decorative pieces. In addition, they had managed to smash the ornate windows and steal the chalices used in the holy sacrament. To further desecrate the churches, they rode their horses into the sanctuaries that became latrines for both men and beasts.

The condemned men followed the wagon up the slope of Benbulbin's prow to the Gully of Ascension. There the timbers were loaded on their backs. Finn and Odhran, like the others, struggled under the weight of the heavy wood that soon became unbearable on their way up the rain-soaked slope of the mountain. On more than one occasion, a condemned man slipped under the weight of the wood only to be grabbed by another. Sir Longford did not want to lose any men prior to their being hung.

Upon reaching the summit, the condemned men formed a single file procession as they proceeded to the prow of the barren mountain. There they were ordered to prepare the scaffolding adjacent to the precipitous edge of Benbulbin. Cromwell wanted them as close to the edge as possible so that travelers could see all seven on clear days.

John, a friend and condemned prisoner, looked at both Odhran and Finn and shouted in Irish, "Forget us not who lived under the tyranny of the English yet died as Irishmen."

Then suddenly, one of the condemned men called loudly in Irish, "Deo in Eirinn!" With that shout, the men leaped to their deaths on the rocky slope below.

Finn shouted, "No! No!" He too lunged towards the edge of the cliff. Only Odhran, holding him back, prevented his death.

THE SOUNDS OF THE SEA STRIKING THE HULL and the shrill call of the wind within the rigging, stirred him from his deep sleep.

"Odhran, you have forgotten what we heard before the battle, those the English do not slaughter will become slaves." They could not have known that they were to join 50,000 Irishmen as well as Scotsmen and Welch in Barbados to work in the plantations of that small island lost in the Caribbean Sea.

Cromwell felt that the Irish were of no more value to him than the Africans that were harvested in the Arab slave trade. It did not matter that the Irish were not well suited to survive in the tropics. Their light-colored skin could not protect them from the relentless rays of the sun. Their true home, Ireland, was one of cold and rain, their native mood too often one of somber reality.

Finn and Odhran quickly found themselves helping in the ship's galley, a reward for their good conduct. It was the only time they were not locked in the creaking wet hole of the ship, a place of petulance and rodents. This respite from the dampness and decay of the ship's hole gave them hope – for in the fresh breezes of the ocean was a sense of freedom.

The ship's cat had been washed overboard early in the voyage allowing the rats and mice to freely forage about the vessel. In addition, the constant odor of pitch and tar from the boatswain's locker irritated their lungs.

The ocean waves baptized their skin now covered with boils. The fresh air relieved the stench of the hold, the salt water felt cool upon their burning flesh. Their joints had previously ached from scurvy but now in the galley, they ate the rind of limes, lemons and later the cores of discarded apples. Due to the hard labor and lack of sufficient food, they soon became even leaner than they were before boarding the HMS *Wales* in Inishbofin. They burned and tanned in the sea breezes, their muscles becoming firmer as they holystoned the decks of the warship.

AFTER TWO MONTHS AT SEA while the frigate chased ghost ships in the vagrant mists of the North Atlantic, they neared the land of the western sea. While still locked in the dark hole of the brig, they felt the interruption of the motion of the ship. They had grown accustomed to the rise and fall of the ship on the large ocean swells. They knew that the rhythm of the waves had changed, and that land must be nearby.

Bare feet running on the oaken deck above them sounded loudly in the small space of their confinement. They looked at one another not knowing whether they should be afraid or happy that the voyage across the sea had ended. They had no idea of what the island would look like or what their future would be. They knew that they were lucky to have not been hung on Benbulbin with their mates. They had heard the others plotting their escape; such knowledge not reported was punishable by death. The condemned had save both Finn and Odhran's lives by their silence.

Soon the master chief of the brig led them to the deck. It was filled with the excitement of English sailors who longed for the pleasures of the shore. Men who had been sullen for days now smiled and joked with one another. They knew whom to stay clear off, those with short tempers and officers looking for additional hands for work that must be performed aboard whether at sea or on land. The brothels promised nights of pleasure, the cost be damned.

"Irishmen, help the crew with the number one windlass. Hurry to the task!" shouted the boatswain's mate of the watch to both Finn and Odhran. Soon the wooden stakes were inserted into the iron drum as the large canvas sails were lowered. "Now heave like Englishmen!"

A chant aided the sailors in the process of lowering the acres of salt-encrusted canvas, ensuring that the men worked in unison, forgetting the pain in their muscles as they heaved about the windlass.

There before them was the clear, aqua-blue of the Caribbean Sea whose true color was that of the atmosphere above it, hues that varied with the angle of the sun's rays. Clouds gave birth to color while gentle rain changed the tone of the reflected light, the salt slowly being washed from their bodies only to be replaced by their own sweat. In the distance were rainbows, some of which touched both land and sea.

They had been fortunate in their approach to the harbor. Sandbars too often fooled a ship's captain with the passing of a cloud, the shallow sea appearing as deep blue water. A vessel was frequently lost in grounding, as were their crews that often did not know how to swim.

Before their eyes, the land was covered in a patchwork of greens concealed by the smoke of burning fields where the stalks of sugarcane had been set ablaze so that new plants might flourish from the ash. The original cover of trees and vines had long since been cleared to make way for sugarcane, cotton and other crops of monetary value. There was no attempt to conserve the natural beauty of the island, but only the desire to exploit the moment of opportunity.

"You two Irish lads, yes, you two, report to the quarterdeck immediately," shouted a petty officer. "The Captain wants to talk to you both."

THEY STOOD BEFORE THE CAPTAIN without shirts, hats or shoes. The ship's commanding officer continued to pace as he talked, "You two have done good work on the ship. I am willing to take you both on as ship's company if you are willing to serve on an English man-of-war." Such an offer was indeed rare but several of the captain's crew members had fallen ill on the voyage and needed to be replaced as the ship was to quickly depart for St. Lucia. There she was to engage the French in a never-ending conflict between the two super powers of the 17th century.

"No, sir. I cannot serve the tyrant Cromwell!" said Finn loudly. Odhran too nodded his head in agreement with Finn's words.

"Then be damned," replied the Captain. "As long as you both were on my ship, you had my protection. Ashore, may God have mercy on you." The Captain looked towards the petty officer in charge of the brig. "Take these two Irishmen to Hunter's Field plantation. Mr. Renfro will enjoy their company. After a day working in the sugarcane fields, they will wish they had accepted my offer."

THEIR HANDS WERE ONCE MORE SECURELY BOUND with leather straps. They were led to the wharf, one leg of each man secured by a common chain. As they stood in the heat, the African slaves emerged from the hole of the ship. At first, they covered their eyes, raising the chains that bound their hands. They had not seen the sun in several weeks. All of the slaves were thin and many found it difficult to stand. Others had distended bellies. Their faces expressed the terror of the unknown.

Among the last to leave the HMS *Wales* was a beautiful young woman. Her appearance made her unique among the slaves. She looked like the painting of an Ethiopian that Finn had seen at an art exhibit while considering Trinity University in Dublin for his studies. The Arabs did not care what sort of people they enslaved as long as there was profit to be made. Beauty was of little value in the sugarcane fields of Barbados. Like life itself, it would not last long in the fields.

Both Finn and Odhran stared at her as she was walked unsteadily down the gangplank to the pier to stand among the rest of the ship's unholy cargo. She too was bound like the other slaves, yet unshackled to another. Separate and apart, she stood alone in the hot sun. She looked down at the planked wharf where she stood. Then as though remembering her position among the slaves, she raised her head and appeared regal in her posture.

An English Marine addressed them all, "The Captain has determined that each of you will be assigned to Hunter's Field in order for you to learn obedience. The master of the plantation does not hesitate to hang rebellious slaves."

Finn found it ironic that he was addressing a group of slaves that could not understand any of his words, only his mannerisms. As the Marine spoke, he repeatedly struck his left hand with a small riding stick.

THE SLAVES WERE SOON TAKEN BY OX CART to an open stockade where they were to live until they died, for there was no place to escape to except to other remote islands in the Caribbean Sea. Their shelters were made of palm fronds and bamboo. Their food consisted of vegetables, fruit, fish and pork, soon to become the traditional food of the Caribbean. There was no attempt to separate the slaves based on their nationality or sex. They were to live and die in a communal experience.

The owner of Hunter's Field, a Simon Renfro, Esq., knew the dangers that threatened his way of life. He had made his way from England to Virginia to work in one of the trading houses located in Norfolk, Virginia. Soon his brilliance and work habits gained him the favor of the company and later the governor of the colony. From there, he was sent to Barbados where he might further serve the crown. He was known as a man who scorned the weakness of others. Simon only believed in himself and none other.

Though he enjoyed great wealth, unease rested upon his disposition. At any moment, the French or Dutch could invade or the torn sails of a marauding pirate ship could appear in the harbor where a quick raid might net her master a hefty bounty of treasure that could not be hidden by the local inhabitants in time. Simon reasoned that the slaves would join anyone that opposed his own way of life. Those that engaged in rebellion were to be hung; those that hinted at it, to be slowly starved or worked so hard that they would surely die within a short period of time.

The wealthy English were becoming used to political turmoil. Charles I had been executed while Cromwell fought the Irish and Welch in costly battles. Finn wondered if "HMS" was even the proper prefix for a Cromwellian ship of the line. Perhaps it was a carryover from the past.

While not in the frequented paths of tropical hurricanes, it was not unusual for Barbados to be occasionally swept by storms. The seas surrounding the island were favored by the swift, shallow draft vessels of marauders who sought safety in the chain of islands that stretched from South America to Florida. If wealth was to be acquired, brutality was necessary. The deathbed was for repentance in the presence of a priest. The moment for profit was now.

THE TROPICAL SUN BEAT DOWN upon the slaves working in the fields. The sugarcane was difficult to plant and harvest, its sharp leaves cut the hands of the careless. Indigenous poisonous snakes found abundant cover in the thick undergrowth and in the shallow mango swamps. Yet in the warm soft glow of twilight, melodic songs from Africa could be heard as the clouds above them wore myriad shades of color.

Matts, barriers for domestic animals and thatch were made from the tall cane, while the sugar content was to be sold abroad, the waste to be fed to livestock. Boiling houses converted the cane to sugar; the product was then shipped in the form of molasses to ports throughout the world. The triangular trade was the stimulant needed to acquire great wealth.

AS THEY SLASHED THE SUGARCANE, Finn looked at the beautiful woman who had arrived with him several weeks earlier. "Do you speak English?" he asked.

She did not reply but continued to chop the sugarcane with a heavy cutlass as the sinews in her arms rippled in the intense sun.

"I said, do you speak English?" he asked again trying not to raise his voice since the foreman was nearby.

"Yes," she replied, not looking at him.

"I am very surprised. I thought my question to be a very foolish one," replied Finn. "How did you learn such a difficult language? Were you a domestic in a landed estate?"

"There was an Irish priest in our city. I attended his school. It was there that I was converted to the religion of the priest."

"How were you captured?" asked Finn. "You seem so different from the others."

"The slave traders came in the night and took me. They thought that since my father was an elder in Filwoha, he had money to pay them for my safe return. He paid them what they asked, but they kept me as a prisoner anyway."

"You are very fair to look upon," Finn said, sweat stinging his eyes as he continued to cut the cane.

"I am no longer pretty." She looked at him and smiled for the first time since he had seen her on the dock. "You are so sunburnt. I know it must hurt."

"Yes, it does. What is your name?" asked Finn.

"My name is very difficult to say in your language. The priest called me Manuela. That is the name that I now have."

"Manuela – that is a very pretty name," Finn said quietly. "I hope that someday you are free and can return to your home."

"I have very little hope of that. During the voyage, I found out from another captive that my city was burned and my parents killed by the Arab slave traders." She then stood erect and looked towards the distant low hills. "These green fields are now my home. I must accept that."

"Don't be so certain of your fate. The Africans, Irish, Welch and Scotch prisoners in Barbados far outnumber the English. Anything is possible. My own country has never been free of the cursed foreigners. We have been slaves since Ireland was called Hibernia by the Romans."

"Don't ever say that you will seek freedom. Don't even think of it! If you rebel, the English will put you to death. If you succeed in taking Barbados, Cromwell's ships will come with many troops. They will not give up Barbados."

He looked at her. "A cause is lost when you think it to be so. Talk to the friends that you trust most about rebellion. There are many who long to be free. We could capture one of the English vessels, set the rest on fire, and sail to Africa." Continuing to cut the sugarcane with his cutlass, he added, "On our passage here, I studied the ship and how the sails were put to good use. Besides, we would be gone before the alarm could be sounded in the Caribbean. There are several stout vessels at the quays in Bridgetown capable of great speed."

He paused for a moment. "I noticed how the other slaves treated you when you left the ship. You are a person of great influence, perhaps even a goddess in their sight."

"And what are you but a poor Irishman? No, a poor Irish boy," she said, smiling. "Because I look and speak differently, they assume I am a person of great importance, a princess of my city or a soothsayer with magical powers. I am none of these things."

"If we revolt, will they follow you? They too must be desperate to return home."

"I will not lead them into hell," Manuela replied looking directly into Finn's eyes. Her long black hair swayed with the warm wind.

"I would not expect that of you. Only if victory can be assured, would I ask you to encourage them," he said in the manner of a proud, young man.

She did not reply but only looked towards the brilliant color of the sun as it neared the surface of the distant sea.

FINN KNEW THAT HER BEAUTY CAPTIVATED HIM. His hatred for

those who enslaved both him and Ireland, however, still dominated his thoughts. Finn was torn between desire and revenge. He wondered if it was possible to have both.

When the sun touched the rising swells of the Caribbean Sea, they returned to their thatched-roof huts. The thought of her made the field work not as laborious, his sunburn less painful. He did not want to fall in love with her. No, he must not fall in love with her. Within his heart, he knew there was little chance of success in winning their freedom; perhaps he could gain her love.

In the coolness of the hut, Finn looked at Odhran. "We must try to leave this island. If we do not, we will surely die here from pestilence or by the hangman's noose. Our best chance for escape is to steal a small sailboat tied along the wharf in the town of Saint Michael. From there, we can sail to Martinique to be liberated by the French."

"Finn, I will not follow you. Do you think the French have any less need for slaves than the English? Even if the French welcome us, there is no chance that we can make our way home. If we are caught and we surely would be, we will stand trial for piracy for stealing a boat. There is only one sentence for piracy that can be given. Our life here is not good, but we are alive. Perhaps Cromwell will be killed and a just monarchy established. Everything can change in a moment. We must be patient."

In the latter part of the following week, Finn saw Manuela once more in the sugarcane field. He walked quickly to where she was partially hidden by the tall reeds. With a surprised look on her face, she turned towards him. "Finn, I have not seen you for several days. I prayed to the Virgin that you were safe and had not acted upon your silly thoughts. Some of us are not destined to be free.

You, like all of us, must accept your fate. The will of God cannot be altered."

He ignored her comment. "See, your prayers have been answered. I have not escaped because I did not want to leave you." As he spoke, he noticed how thin she had become, even more so than when he had first seen her. "Are you being given enough food?"

"Yes, but I feel weak. I don't know what is wrong. I am not used to hard work. Perhaps that is the answer. Even though my skin is dark, my energy is taken by the sun."

"Are you eating fruits and vegetables? On the HMS *Wales*, the sailors talked of a sickness called 'scurvy' that resulted from not eating fruit. To prevent the disease, their officers made them eat dark-colored fruit. I was lucky enough to eat the waste of the fruit left over from the officer's mess."

"There are no vegetables or fruit available to us that are dark in color," she said. "We have only broth from the fat of hogs and fish to eat. Nothing more."

"Manuela, there are fruit trees in the tyrant's orchid. I will take what has fallen to the ground and give them to you. It will not taste good, but it will save your life."

THAT NIGHT FINN SLIPPED OVER THE HIGH GARDEN WALL that was fashioned from coral and, with his hands, felt for the soft, overly ripened fruit that lay scattered on the ground. He stuffed his pockets with what he could find and quickly climbed the wall just as the master's dogs began to bark. He soon heard voices as Simon Renfro's overseer and servants searched for intruders, their torches glowing in the night sky.

The next morning he spied Manuel walking slowly towards the cane field. "I have some fruit for you." He reached into his pockets and pulled out an overly ripened mango and a small unripe grapefruit. "Take these and eat everything including the rind." She reached for the fruit, hands shaking. He sensed inwardly that if they did not escape from the island, she would soon die. He could not continue to steal fruit from the garden without being caught. Finn knew that if he was captured, he would be hanged as a thief. There would be no mercy for a slave that had entered the gated area of Master Renfro's house.

EACH DAY AS THEY WERE LED TO THE FIELDS, he looked at the wharf and sandy beach. A few large fishing boats were firmly secured with chains along the quay while several small island skiffs were laid carelessly upon the beach. Many lacked maintenance and were partially filled with fresh rainwater. Other skiffs with their seams open were slowly being covered by the drifts of beach sand.

IN THE EVENING AS THE NIGHT FIRES WERE LIT, Finn quietly walked over to Manuela's hut. He found her lying on a woven mat. Without rising, she looked at him as he approached her. He knelt down beside her, took her hand and whispered, "Can a man love a woman who is but a stranger to him?"

Manuela propped herself on her elbow. She looked at him as the firelight reflected in her eyes, their hands grasping one another's. "Yes, it is possible."

Finn replied, "Perhaps love exists in its purest form when lovers have not touched."

She understood the young Irishman in a manner that words could not convey. A wave of primitive emotion flowed from both their bodies. She tightened her grip on his hand.

"Then I love you, Manuela," he said as he too reclined on the mat beside her. "We should marry even if we are alone beneath a canopy of trees without altar and priest. The jungle animals will hear our vows, for I believe that God dwells in all living things."

She spoke quietly while still tightly holding his hand. "Yes, I will marry you even if only the sky, earth and sea hear our vows." With these words, she moved closer to him on the mat, placing her head in the shelter of his arm. There they looked at the tropical night sky in its array, stars so close that they appeared like moons orbiting the earth. The constellation of Orion seemed to touch both land and sea. Far above, a shower of shooting stars appeared. "See, the God of both of our peoples approve of our love."

He rose to his knees. "Then with the most simple of words, let us be married this very moment." With a smile he softly said, "I, Finn O'Flaherty take you to be my wife this night beneath the stars. I will love and cherish you till time has ceased for me."

Manuela rose to her knees and then took both of his hands. "I, Manuela take you for my husband. To love and cherish you till time has ceased."

"I have no ring for you except the fragment of a shell. May I place it upon your finger?" Earlier, Finn had seen the shell of a small mollusk in the sand of a stream that flowed from the hill above them. It was a thin shell with a perfectly round opening in the center. He had kept it as a reminder that beauty exists. Later he had intended to give it to her as a necklace. Instead this night, he placed it gently upon her finger.

"We are now together forever. Neither time nor tyranny can separate us."

They both rose and walked towards a small stream that ran from the hillside where the tropical vegetation was still dense, one of the few remaining virgin growths of palms and other indigenous plants.

There they knelt once more and together they joined in an embrace that was to last forever. Wild birds called within the jungle and the sound of the flowing water joined the lovers. He entered her not as a conqueror but as a gentle lover, caring more for her than for himself.

The next morning before the sun had risen above the fields of sugarcane, they embraced once more, then let their hands fall from one another's. After a final kiss, they walked silently in the direction of their shelters.

THE FOLLOWING NIGHT, FINN LOOKED FOR ODHRAN. "We three have to escape. In the night, security appears to be lax along the beachfront. There is a small boat that has been pulled upon the sand. It has a lateen sail still attached to the mast. There is even a water keg stored in the bilge. I am certain that it will carry us safely to Martinique. If we time our escape carefully, we might just make it."

Odhran looked at Finn in amazement. "What do you mean, we three have to escape? Who is the third person?"

"Manuela. We are now married."

"You cannot be serious." He laughed. "There is no priest to marry you, no church, no sacrament to bless you."

"What need have we of man's institutions? They have only brought us war and poverty. I obeyed my heart and we exchanged vows last night in the forest. The night was our priest. Whatever god rules us, he heard our vows. Regardless of our different cultures, we are one now."

"Finn, like I said when we first arrived in Barbados, I am not willing to take the chance of escaping. You shouldn't either. Our lives are short enough." After a lengthy pause, Odhran continued, "Two slaves marrying one another. "Don't you miss our home in Drogheda? Do you not long for your family and the pretty young girl that you loved?"

Odhran then paused. "I guess that your marrying another now makes as much sense as any of this does. I wish you could have been married in Drogheda, but then in truth we will never see Ireland again. I do not expect any of us to live long, so what harm is there in having a dream?"

Finn and Odhran embraced one another.

"Of course, I miss my home but what good is a dream? We are thousands of miles from Ireland. The Atlantic is no soft mistress. She kills whom she will," Finn said as he looked seaward towards the rising of the moon.

THROUGHOUT THE DAY THE WIND DECREASED until the air felt humid and oppressive. Above the sea, high altitude clouds were moving swiftly in a northwesterly direction. As the evening progressed, thick cumulus clouds hid the moon. Rain fell in heavy downburst and then abruptly stopped. The sound of the surf increased in intensity as did the wind. Finn sensed that somewhere to the southeast a great storm was being given birth.

In the twilight of a tropical morning, Finn noticed that the small skiff had been pulled higher on a sand dune. Its sail now furled about the mast that lay upon the deck of the boat. Then without another word or a moment of hesitation, perhaps totally from the instinct to be free, Finn and Manuela pushed the skiff from the shore and boarded her. Their hearts beat loudly within their chests. The winds were increasing in speed and the clouds moving quickly above their heads. The tops of the tallest clouds appeared to be supporting a ceiling made of a different type of cloud formation. Bands of rain began to fall about them. Manuela smiled at Finn as the warm rain ran down her face.

Finn looked at Manuela. "At last we are free. Let us pray that the sea is more forgiving than our master will be if we are caught." Just as he spoke, the sun broke free of the sea.

THE SMALL CRAFT RODE THE TOWERING SWELLS as their vessel raced towards the coast of Martinique, a hundred and forty-two miles to the north. They knew that they would need to stand clear of St. Lucia since the British now controlled the island. If they sought shelter there, they would be returned in chains to Barbados where they would await a trail for piracy. It would be better to perish together at sea than to be hung together on Bridgetown's wharf as a warning to the slaves of the island. Like the condemned men who had chosen to leap from Benbulbin's summit, they too would choose death rather than capture.

The small vessel was but a mere speck on the ocean as the hurricane approached the coast of Barbados. From the crests of the towering cliffs of water, the small boat fell into the troughs of the steep waves. Spume filled the air as he once more felt the need to reduce sail. Finn lowered the jib and reefed the mainsail. He sought only enough canvas to maintain steerage. Finn knew that they should now be running bare pole before the wind, having cast their sails and other equipment overboard to serve as a sea anchor with the intent being to point the bow into the wind. Instead he rode the waves as though born to the breezes, now defiant to both man and nature.

"What island do I see off our beam?" shouted Finn as blowing spume blurred his vision.

"There are two volcanic cones that look like a woman's breasts," she replied.

"Do you know the name of the island?" Finn shouted once more, salt stinging his eyes.

"It must be St. Lucia," Manuela replied shouting through her cupped hands.

"How do you know that?" he asked.

"A slave from St. Lucia mentioned it to me. He had been sold to our master as punishment for his rebellious nature," she answered loudly above the scream of the wind. "Martinique is the island just to the northwest of St. Lucia."

JUST THEN A GRAYBEARD POUNDED THE STERN of the boat. The vessel yawed violently and fell into the trough of the passing wave. Both Manuela and Finn bailed as quickly as they could. They both sensed that Martinique was too far away from their reach. To turn the vessel towards Saint Lucia where they might have sought refuge until the storm passed, they would have been presenting their beam to the waves that would ensure a capsize.

"Hold tight to me!" shouted Finn into the wind.

Only her lips replied above the roar of the sea, "I love you."

Finn shouted back, "We shall always be together though the gods protest that it is not to be so!"

THE MORNING SUN SWEPT ACROSS A SILENT SEA. Only the large swells remained of the nameless storm.

CHAPTER TWO

Castaway

SIMONE HAD WANDERED FAR FROM THE PLANTATION. As she walked, she thought about her life with Philippe Degas, how romantic it had been in Paris. The walks through the parks and the moments spent in the sidewalk cafés of the Boulevard Montmartre drinking the excellent wines of southern France. At first, the island of Martinique sounded like a great adventure. Philippe and Simone were young and madly in love. Philippe described the island to her as being a tropical paradise in which a young man could make a fortune in coconuts, sugarcane and the slave trade.

Now more than ever, she realized how incomplete her life had become since arriving in Martinique. It was a mere dot in the vast oceans of the world. An island of only 420 square miles. The difference between winter and summer were but a few humid degrees. There were no opera houses, no museums, nor any works of art. The streets, unlike those of Paris, were but dirt roads. Even the beach was colored by the ash of the smoldering volcano, Mont Pelée. Her only social acquaintances were women who found themselves in similar circumstances. Their weekly meeting at the Parisian Club in Saint-Pierre was her only respite from the monotony of her life.

Philippe spent all of his time in his office in the small town of Schoelcher. His businesses, as well as the fruits of the plantation, were yielding great profits. He was also busily engaged in an attempt to grow coffee in the higher regions of the island. When he returned late in the evenings, he would retire to his study. When not working, he would look out over the sea to St. Lucia, an island now in the possession of the British, a sworn enemy of France.

More than once the island of Martinique had been invaded by the British. Their villa had even been hit by a bombardment from the HMS *Invasion*. Yet they rebuilt, using the labor of slaves and indentured servants.

On the morning of her stroll, she walked further than she ever had before. The smell of the sea was strong. She walked barefoot on the sandy beach, careful to avoid sharp shell fragments and hard stones.

Even though she and Philippe tried to have a child, a future heir to the estate, she could not get pregnant. As she rounded the cliff that led to the beach, she saw before her a small distant object, alone on the sand. Mist from the breaking waves at first obscured a clear view. Nearby was the wreckage of a British pulling boat. There were three dead black slaves lying on the sand, apparently shot by the British after they had attacked them with only the most primitive of weapons.

As she neared the unidentified object, a young child could be heard crying above the sounds of the breaking waves. She ran to where the infant was sitting in the warm waters of the sea. Small waves broke upon his back. To her it seemed so strange, like an unexpected gift cast by the waves. She studied him, afraid to touch the small, frail body. He was dark complexioned yet his features appeared not to be that of an African slave. There was no baby fat about his cheeks. His hair was wavy. What were most unusual about him were his eyes. They were as blue green as a shallow sea.

Around his neck was the handwoven cross of Saint Bridget. As she looked at him, he cried and extended his arms to her. She could not resist. Her heart pounded in her chest. She reached down and picked up the naked child who cried even more loudly. She turned and ran with him towards her villa. She was breathing heavily when she spied the plantation house in the distance. Even though not fully understood by her, she felt such love for this child cast from the sea.

As she neared the veranda of the large, single story white house that was surrounded by a broad porch, she called loudly, "Maria, Maria, be quick!"

The young cousin who had just arrived from Brittany for a three-month visit appeared on the veranda. "Simone, what have you in your arms? Have you found a child?"

"Yes, yes, I found this infant sitting in the sand more than two miles from here. I don't know what possessed me to walk so far today. Perhaps it was the Virgin Mary who directed my footsteps."

"What will you do with the baby?" her cousin asked.

"I don't know. Her parents were obviously killed or taken prisoner by the British. There were bodies strewn nearby but they did not look like the parents of this child. I did not bother to try to identify any of the dead. I imagine that they were runaway slaves living at the source of the stream flowing from the mountain. To be honest, I was too afraid of being set upon by either slave or British marine."

Simone immediately dispatched a servant to fetch her husband who was busy in Saint-Pierre. It was not long before her husband's boots could be heard running towards her. "Simone, what on earth is going on? Malon said you had a small baby in your arms. Is it the child of one of our friends?"

Simone turned towards him and removed the swaddling clothes that covered the child. There before him was a beautiful young boy. When he looked at Philippe, the unknown infant smiled revealing his beautiful Caribbean sea-colored eyes.

That evening after the child had been fed by a wet nurse, they sat upon the veranda watching the sun as it descended into the tropical clouds above a still ocean. "I will find a slave to take the child."

"No, I want the baby to be our own! The sea and Saint Bridget gave him to me. When I picked him up, he was holding a small scallop shell in his left fist. I will name him Samuel Shell. Samuel was a gift from God and so is this young child. I have so much love to give and God has now blessed me at an age when I can no longer hope of having a son."

TOO SOON SAMUEL GREW INTO A HANDSOME YOUNG MAN. In his late teens, his mother asked him to meet her on the porch as the setting sun sat the clouds aflame. "Samuel, it is time for you to travel to Paris for a proper education. You must learn the manners of a gentleman and the knowledge of a businessman. Someday this estate will be yours to manage. You must be well taught. I will give you a letter of introduction to my cousin. She will be responsible for ensuring your safety and education."

TEN YEARS LATER SAMUEL RETURNED TO MARTINIQUE. He had been a brilliant student at La Sorbonne located in the Latin Quarter. A place where universities converged among cafés and cabarets. The voices of scholars, debaters and students mixed with the sounds of pianos and violins. Wine and passion flowed freely in the 5th and 6th arrondissements of Paris.

Samuel had fallen in love with Sophie Michel, a young beauty whose father was a classical language scholar at the Sorbonne. Her black hair, dark eyes and soft skin intoxicated him. Into the morning hours, they made love above the noisy street below them. It was as though their shutters could isolate them from the lively atmosphere and bistros beneath their windows.

It was mid-afternoon when Sophie suggested that they dine at Café Le Procope. Le Procope was one of the premier restaurants in Paris. Many famous guests had eaten there. Among them were Lieutenant Bonaparte, Hugo and Voltaire. The perfect setting for two wealthy young people in love.

That evening Sophie wore a dress of oriental motif, a popular design in 19th-century France. In her hair were red roses; about her neck were multiple strings of pearls. Attached to her waist was also a garland of pink and red roses. Her long gloves matched the exotic nature of her gown. The moment she entered Café Le Procope, every gentleman gave her prolonged glances. The women wondered where she had obtained such a striking gown that accented the loveliness of her body.

No sooner had they been seated than Monsieur Henri Vertaine approached their table. Henri was a classmate of Samuel's. They were both preparing for the bar. Often in class, they would clash over differing points of view in order to impress their instructor and to intimidate the more timid students.

"Well, look who is here with such a stunning woman," said the intoxicated Henri.

"Henri, is it not enough that I must bear your tedious nature in class?" responded Samuel. Sophie smiled at both gentlemen acknowledging what she assumed to be their playful, combative natures.

Henri looked at Sophie. "Why are you with this man whose father is a slave trader?"

Samuel pushed his chair back from the heavy table. "Sir, you must not mention my father in such terms. He is a gentleman of the highest order. I must remind you that slavery is legal under French law. Do you think that their lives would be better off in Africa than in Martinique?"

"You will not cow me down when we both know the horror that men like your father have brought upon an entire continent. What man, when given the choice, would not choose freedom?" he shouted so loudly that the entire restaurant became quiet.

Matching his voice, Samuel said, "I suggest that you restate your opinion now, for later I will not accept an apology."

Both men were wearing small daggers in their waistbands. Henri unsheathed his weapon and held it before Samuel who in turn took the serving knife from the table top and lunged at Henri, who deflected the blow away from his heart. Henri however had been cut and was bleeding profusely from the wound.

The stunned café owner shouted, "Juliette, quickly, get a surgeon. The poor gentleman may yet be saved!"

Samuel took Sophie's arm and quickly led her out. Shortly thereafter, Samuel planned to leave for Brittany. He did not know the condition of Henri nor did he care. If he died, Samuel would be brought before the judge; if he lived, Samuel would be forced to leave the Sorbonne.

He knew that Sophie would never consent to live in Martinique. The night before his departure, they stood before the waiting carriage. She handed him a rose from her hair as the carriage door closed.

As he debarked from the brigantine in the town of Saint-Pierre, he felt good. He was home. The swaying coconut fronds and the sounds of the white-breasted tremblers were reminders that he had returned to the island that he loved.

He now not only spoke Latin, but also German and English, languages necessary for world trade. As the carriage neared his father's estate, his heart quickened. In the distance he could see his mother sitting on the veranda. He leaped from the carriage and ran towards her.

Simone's eyes had faded with time. She shouted to a servant, "Who comes towards me running?"

The servant, who had never seen Samuel before, told her, "Madam, I have no idea. He is young and very handsome."

"Mother, Mother," Samuel shouted.

"My son, my son, you have returned!"

"Where is Papa?" Samuel asked as he held her tightly.

"He is dead, Samuel. He was so proud of you. The blessed Father has kept us all informed regarding your accomplishments."

Samuel knew that the priest had not told her why he had to depart Paris so quickly. At that point, Samuel knelt before her and wept.

That evening as they sat together for the first time in ten years, his mother put her hand upon his own. "Samuel the estate is now yours. Manage it as your father would have. He loved you very much."

"I know he did and I him. I have been blessed far more than I can ever repay."

"Samuel, the British remain our enemy. Privateers and pirates still seek targets of opportunity. You must always be careful. I have arranged to have a social function here at the house to welcome you home. There are many beautiful daughters of businessmen and plantation owners who will be very happy to meet you."

THE NIGHT OF THE PARTY, SAMUEL WAS DRESSED in a most handsome suit that he had acquired in Paris. His mother had been correct, there were many beautiful women for him to dance with. One in particular caught his attention, a Maria D'Ora. Her father had been a friend of his own father. After being introduced to her at the ball, he sought every occasion to be with her.

One evening while strolling along the beach, their conversation became more intimate.

"Your mother told me all about you," said Maria.

"As you probably know, I do not know who my real family is," he responded.

"Your real family is here."

"Yes, you are correct, yet I feel that something is missing. There is a longing in me that I cannot explain. Often in Paris, I had dreams of my birth mother. I could never see her face. Strange, the most important part of a person, I could not see."

"She or your father must have been Irish. Your adopted mother told me that you were wearing a handwoven cross of reeds, Saint Bridget's cross, I think. Only a father or mother who was from Ireland would have woven such a cross. Also, your most distinguishing trait, your blue-green eyes, tells me you have Celtic blood."

"Perhaps you are right," Samuel said holding her tightly. He knew he was falling in love far too quickly. His father had financial dealings with Monsieur D'Ora that involved the lucrative slave trade.

Because of the British patrols, North America was off limits to the French trade. South America, however, needed increasing numbers of slaves. It was a common practice for many of the French slaves to be sold on the black market to British slave traders in nearby St. Lucia.

Samuel had often wondered if his parents had been captured in Martinique and taken to the slave market on the island of the Pitons, St. Lucia. As he sat on his veranda, he looked at the distant island.

No more had Samuel returned to Martinique and married, than the Battle of Martinique occurred, a naval and land engagement between the two super powers of the time, France and Britain. He knew he was the son of a slave, whether the master was French or British. As a result of this knowledge, he and his holdings remained neutral during the war. Soon the British flag flew over the island.

Samuel knew that while a coin has two sides, it remains only one coin. For the next twenty years, the British ruled, only turning the island back over to the French in 1815. A date that coincided with the conclusion of the Napoleonic Wars.

With his knowledge of the slave trade and a variety of unique commodities, he felt that a lucrative business could be developed between Charleston and Martinique. His only son and heir was born aboard the barkentine *Queen of the Seas* bound for South Carolina. It was upon the seas that a new Samuel Shell was born.

CHAPTER THREE
A Time of War and Fortune

No Victory for Mortal Man

Who are these that I have defeated,
Are they not the spoils of war?
They are without name and friendly face.

The end of war a victory secure
The dead lie alone while birds sing,
A blue sky and sharp winter wind that stings

What do I know but war?
Shall I not continue to command the weak?
One does not win against thy self.

Another struggle to ensure.
A new enemy to engage.
Forever searching to build and destroy.

IT WAS THE FALL OF 1864. The Confederacy was running short of all things essential to war. The threat of a hard winter hung over the beleaguered forces of General Hood who were retreating from the Battle of Franklin. The Little River had already begun to have small drifts of ice cascading over Desoto Falls. Low water halted the Coosa River traffic that now clustered downstream from where the battle had occurred.

The remnants of the once proud Southern army were defeated after they ran out of ammunition and food. The starvation of the troops finally ended the brief siege. The starving forces, largely formed of young boys and drafted old men, were too weak to charge with bayonets alone. They sat silently in their hastily dug trenches awaiting capture. Their will to fight was lost.

Colonel Samuel Shell won the skirmish, and that was all that mattered. He did not want to hear any complaints from the prisoners regarding their need for food or warmth in the frigid weather. He marched them over the newly frozen soil. Many went barefoot. Some lost their crude homemade shoes during the siege, others had them stripped off their feet by the victorious Union soldiers who needed to warm their own feet.

WHEN FOUR MEN ATTEMPTED TO ESCAPE, they were quickly caught and taken before the Union Colonel.

"I understand that you attempted to escape, thereby endangering my own troops in the pursuit. As I said earlier, the penalty for putting my men at risk is hanging." Colonel Shell looked at the second lieutenant who stood rigidly beside him. "Hang them now."

The war ended too soon for the Colonel to make general. He knew that if General Robert E. Lee had not surrendered at

Appomattox, it would have been only a matter of time until he received his first star. That promotion would have ensured his place on any corporate board following the war. "Too bad that Sherman didn't get his way. The Union Army should have burned the South to ashes even after Lee presented his sword," he said to his staff before they were discharged from active duty.

AT THE END OF THE WAR, Colonel Shell moved to California. He sensed that there were huge profits to be made regardless of what part of the country he settled in. The South was ripe for the taking since there was little political structure in place and, therefore, presented the most modest of challenges to him. Those who were elected to office by a disenfranchised population could easily be manipulated. The West, however, was where the challenge was and the greatest of fortunes to be made.

He had invested his money wisely in both railroads and gold shares. He knew it would not be difficult to make a fortune in California for Chinese labor was cheap and readily available for the building of a spur line off the Great Northern Railway. The spur line would open up more of the Sierras to mining and land speculation. He would acquire land prior to the building of the spur knowing that property could be purchased for virtually nothing. Indian land was largely free to those who lay claim to it.

He did not care how the land was acquired. The Colonel did not ask his agents for details nor did he question their accountability before the law.

IN HIS OFFICE IN SACRAMENTO, the Colonel welcomed his railroad foreman.

"Come in Mr. King, how are things going?" He paused knowing the answer to his own question. "I received your telegraph stating that the coolies are demanding more money. You can tell the bastards that if they do a day's work, they will be paid a day's wage. So far they are proving to be a lazy bunch, to say the least. If they don't like what I am pay'em, tell'm all that they can find work elsewhere. Just remind them also that I can have their lazy asses deported by sending but a single telegram to my associates here in Sacramento. Tell'm that!" He leaned back in his swivel chair and lit a large sweet-smelling cigar. He did not look again at his foreman, but instead stared out his window towards the dry land to the east, the door shutting quietly behind him.

He worked as though his business was a military command. Orders given, to be obeyed without question. Each day was conducted as though he were preparing for a battle. He arose early, dressed smartly and left promptly for his post; a walnut paneled office on the top floor of the five-story Shell Building.

Colonel Shell had acquired the necessary political connections through his friendships with fellow West Point graduates. When California became a state, he was certain that he would be elected as a member of Congress. He had acquired the traits necessary to accumulate both wealth and control over others. To conquer a foe, destroy his will to fight. As he would later say, "Never slack your line when catching a fish, large or small."

He also purchased land in southern California along the coast. It was land that few desired, dry barren soil that led to hills and then beyond the mountains. He did not know why, but he sensed that there was more gold under the dry lands that hugged the coastline. The oil fields of Terminal Island were yet to be discovered. These lands were to later form the nucleus of the Shell family's fortune.

Even though he had earlier married Linda Coleman, daughter of Boston financier Robert Coleman, he spent a great deal of his time drinking and spending every free moment with his mistress, Irish beauty Ruby Hamilton Smith. She had been the daughter of a merchant ship captain, who upon reaching the Los Angeles basin abandoned his ship as well as his family in his desire to mine for gold. With her mother's return to Ireland, she was left to live on her own. Her beauty ensured her future as a saloon girl and later the Colonel's lover.

Even though he should have slept well after each day's success, night after night the Colonel suffered from nightmares: a warm sea entering his lungs, mountains without names and a dark woman with unseen face. While he could dictate commands to others, he could not control the frequency and content of his dreams.

WHILE ENGAGED IN A LAND TRANSACTION in the Sacramento Valley, the Colonel received a telegram from Linda telling him that her father, the banker Judge Coleman was very ill in Boston and desired to see her immediately. She was to travel by train from Sacramento where they had just completed their mansion overlooking the distant Sacramento Valley and the Sierra Mountains.

That evening the Colonel sent word to Ruby to meet him at the Byron Club, an exclusive gentlemen's club in San Francisco two days hence. Since membership was by invitation, only a select number of men were allowed to be members. It was a large red-brick two-story building located in the financial section of the city.

Secrecy was fundamental to the clients since business transactions were often conducted within its rooms. It also had a large ornate bar where men could meet their mistresses for drinks. Wives were not invited nor allowed to enter such a secretive club. Since many members were Irish, some of the men had been associated with the notorious Hell Fire Club located just outside the city of Dublin.

TWO DAYS LATER, RUBY ARRIVED IN SAN FRANCISCO. Immediately she let the Colonel's lawyer know of her arrival, such was the secrecy of their relationship. With news of her arrival, the Colonel concluded his business and traveled by train to San Francisco.

Upon his arrival, the air was cold and damp with sea fog that crept through the streets and parks of the city.

From the train depot, she too had taken a carriage to the Byron Club. As Ruby entered the bar, every man turned to gaze upon her beauty. Her furs concealed the beautiful lavender gown she wore underneath. Her hat was large and stylish as dictated by the current styles seen in Parisian society. The Colonel rose from his chair and softly kissed her extended hand.

"Thank you for joining me. As you know from my telegraph, Mrs. Shell has traveled to be with her ailing father in Boston. I received a telegram from her just today saying that she would not return to California until her father regains his strength. This is a perfect time for me to travel by steamer to Oahu. A fellow officer and West Point graduate who now lives there has married into one of the Mormon missionary families that have managed to buy much of the native Hawaiian land. He would like for me to invest with him in some agricultural projects, you know, sugar and pineapples. There are also some additional incentives to invest in ranch land."

"Samuel, what value are cattle thousands of miles away from any respectable civilization?" she asked.

The Colonel did not like to be challenged even in so mild a way. "This is not something that you need to trouble yourself with," he said in a tone that indicated a degree of irritation.

"I am sorry, I should not have asked," replied Ruby with her face now flushing with repressed agitation. She felt that her sense of business was as keen as his, perhaps even more so.

"Well anyway, I would like for you to sail there with me. If we need more than a month, I will tell my wife that the negotiations are progressing slowly, and that I will not know when I will be returning."

Ruby looked intently into Samuel's eyes. "There is something that we must discuss."

The Colonel looked around to ensure that none of his friends could overhear their conversation. He did not know what to expect but her mannerisms indicated that an event of great importance was involved, one that must be shared in silence.

"I am pregnant," she said, holding her stomach to emphasize the importance of her statement.

"What? How? When?" he said much too loudly. Two couples at other tables turned around and looked at him. He quickly acknowledged their stares with the nodding of his head and then looked away from their tables towards Ruby.

"It wasn't my time to ovulate. I can't explain more. It just happened, and that is all that I know," she said.

"Well, that is a problem that can be solved quickly. I will ask Mr. Kent, my attorney to arrange an abortion," he said uneasily.

"I don't want an abortion. I am Catholic. In Purgatory, how can I confront a child that I killed? Especially if it was my own," she said as tears ran down her cheeks.

"What do you want me to do about it? Find you a husband?" he said sarcastically.

"You must marry me!" she demanded.

"Have you lost your mind?" he said in a mocking tone.

"That is your decision regarding how you obtain a divorce," she said with anger in her voice.

"You are asking me to divorce my wife? I thought that was also a sin."

"It is, but my child will not be punished in this life for what I have done. You are a man of wealth and power. Linda never gave you an heir, but I will."

The waiter brought a bottle of burgundy to the table. The wine steward removed the cork and then poured a small amount of wine into a glass for the Colonel to render an opinion regarding the bouquet of the wine. The Colonel looked up at him. "Pour the damn thing and leave the bottle on the table!" he said in a voice full of anger.

AFTER ARRANGING FOR RUBY TO SPEND THE NIGHT at the club, he left the bar and walked out into the brisk air. He sauntered until the fog completed its journey from off the Bay covering the streetlights and row houses on Signal Hill. The fog lingered into the morning. Near the wharfs, the sounds of stevedores could be heard.

The Colonel loved Ruby but not as he would a wife. A relationship with a young mistress was expected of successful men unless it became an item of gossip. Linda could be depended upon. In addition, her father was a prominent member of society with highly placed friends in public office that could be essential to fulfilling his ambitions. Society would never accept his marrying a common bargirl regardless of how beautiful she was.

A WEEK LATER THE COLONEL BOARDED THE LINER *Henry Watts* two days before she was scheduled to sail. She was a small liner that also carried cargo to the islands. Such a vessel would help assure that his journey did not garner undue publicity. She did offer luxurious accommodations for a limited number of guests. A new and fast liner, her freshly painted white superstructure glistened in the sun. Her tall black funnel carried a red palm tree crest indicating that her line was dedicated to the Pacific Islands trade.

The evening before she sailed from San Francisco, Ruby boarded the cargo liner and discretely waited for the Colonel to join her. The steward had already been instructed to take her immediately to his cabin. As he turned the brightly polished brass doorknob, she rose to greet him. There in the secrecy of the cabin they embraced.

After refreshing themselves with several glasses of wine, they were joined by other guests in the main salon for dinner. Seated at another table was a tall, young man with black hair and broad shoulders. The Colonel noticed that Ruby continued to glance in his direction as though she knew him intimately. The young stranger did not return her glances, but continued his conversation with the other guests.

Later, the wardroom steward brought a Tom Collins to the Colonel's table and placed it before Ruby. He also placed a letter in an open envelope beside her sterling silver tableware. Ruby glanced at the stranger. In return, he acknowledged her stare with a brief nod.

Even though the Colonel was well aware of what was occurring, he continued to be engaged in a conversation with an older couple sitting at their table. To show his displeasure would have been to illustrate his weakness.

Ruby was careful not to taste the drink that had been prepared for her. She did, however, place the envelope with its card showing inside her purse. Then she clipped her purse so that it remained invisible.

Even though the Colonel was irate, he did not want to confront Ruby until he had worked out a solution to the problem of her being pregnant. He knew that she had been with many men – any of whom could have been the father of the child. It did not matter. An accusation by her was enough to establish guilt in the powerful, yet fragile society in which he dwelt.

THE NEXT DAY THEY WERE AWAKENED by a variety of noises on the main deck. It was the familiar sounds common to any ship preparing to get underway. A ship's officer in uniform knocked on the cabin door. The Colonel opened it smartly. Through the companionway, he could see a person standing at attention.

"Sir, the ship is preparing to depart. The Captain thought that you and your wife would like a streamer to toss to family and friends on the pier."

"Thank you," replied the Colonel as though addressing one of his field officers.

Later, they stood apart as each cast a streamer ashore. The Colonel's lay unattended on the dock. Two young stevedores picked up Ruby's and waved at her.

She turned towards him. "Colonel, a small victory for me," she said smiling.

THAT EVENING THEY SAT AT THE CAPTAIN'S TABLE, an invitation that all passengers sought. Samuel was dressed in a black tuxedo and black tie just as all of the wealthy in attendance did. Ruby, however was striking in a red velvet gown, so low cut that it showed the beautiful diamond she was wearing. Several ladies shielded their mouths as they whispered audibly to one another, "Do you think that is real?"

The Colonel was very pleased at the attention that Ruby generated. The blue diamond matched the color of her eyes.

The Captain looked at them. "Colonel, it is a great pleasure to meet you and your companion, Ruby. Mr. Frazier of the shipping line *Black Star* had many good things to say about you. He commanded me to treat you special. It seems like the two of you graduated from West Point together. He also mentioned that you both served in the Western Campaign. I admire military men, they are loyal to a cause."

Ruby felt ill at ease. She did not like being called a man's companion. She was just as real as he was and far more noble. Her child deserved so much more than being born a bastard.

The cigar smoke made her feel queasy. She excused herself from the table and quickly walked towards the promenade deck. As she opened the door, a strong gust of wind blew across the tables, which drew immediate attention to her leaving the wardroom.

When she could no longer be seen by the Captain and his guests, she ran past the covered deck and stood against the railing, forcing the stanchion against her stomach. The ship was encased in heavy fog as the frigid waters of the Humboldt Current collided with the warmer waters of the tropical Pacific Ocean. She could hear the sounds of the coal-fed steam engines that propelled the *Henry Watts* thought the ink-black water. She paused and looked down into the impenetrable fog. The deck lights were reflected back into her eyes.

The Colonel rose. "Gentlemen, please excuse me. I must rescue my little one from herself. She has been fraught with anxiety ever since we left San Francisco. I think that the ocean gives her a fright." The Colonel walked slowly to the door before opening it. In the distance, he could see a lone figure leaning precariously against the railing.

I should leap over the side, she thought. *Maybe that will get his attention.* Then she wept loudly. *I will live not for myself but for my child. His life is not mine to take.*

At that moment she felt Samuel's arm go around her waist. "Ruby, you cannot stand in the cold night air. You will catch pneumonia. Come back in and join us again. I realize how difficult it is to be pregnant on a rolling ship. In the future, I will ask the steward to prepare something easier to digest. Perhaps we should dine more often in our stateroom."

She turned towards Samuel. "I thought about ending my life. To end the complications I have created."

"I thought about pushing you over the side," he said with a strange laugh. He paused. "But then who would enjoy Hawaii with me? You know that I need an audience. What good is being a master if you do not have a bondservant?"

"Is that what you think of me?" she asked defiantly.

"No, of course not. I don't know how to classify you. I look at you as more of a business relationship. You provide me with a service, and I pay you richly for it."

"You are describing our relationship as one of indifference."

"Come on, Ruby. I am freezing out here. Let's be honest, you had no intention of jumping, no more than I had of pushing you. As you may have reasoned out, suicide is something you cannot take back. You could not have lasted ten minutes in this frigid water, no one could."

He led her back into the wardroom with his hand tightly about her waist. Ruby knew that he might have wished her dead, but such a death would have created a great deal of gossip, especially if her body was recovered and she was found to be pregnant. Too many witnesses had seen him follow her onto the deck. "If he intends to kill me, he will need to do it with less showmanship." It was only then that she noticed that they could be observed through a large rectangular window.

Ruby did realize that she had laid the framework for her own possible murder. The members of the Captain's table could easily testify to her own anxiety as they had watched her through the window.

The next day, the ship departed the fog bank and entered into the blue-diamond sea of the warm Pacific. Much of their time was spent walking on the promenade deck on the leeward side of the ship. Ruby wanted to remain stylish with her large hat adorned with peacock feathers. The gentle roll of the ship was conducive to lounging on the wicker furniture along the decks frequented by first-class passengers.

While she was seated alone, the man who had purchased her a drink approached and sat down in the empty deck chair next to her.

"Ruby, I can't believe it is you. All the years that have passed since I last saw you in Dublin have not rendered you less beautiful. What are you doing with the Colonel? Don't you know the reputation that man has regarding young women? Don't turn to someone like Colonel Shell. He destroys lives just as readily as he builds financial empires."

"David O'Dea. I cannot believe it is you," she said, smiling. "You know, there was a time when I thought you loved me and only me. You are more dangerous than the Colonel. He is so obvious, but you were not. He steals from others, but you deceive the people who love you. You let me love you while all the time you had a wife in Galway. That is why I sailed with Father, to escape your deception."

"Ruby, how could you believe that? I was not married, only a person who also sought your love told such a lie. I would have followed you to America, but being the oldest son, I had a mother and five siblings to look after."

"Well, David, you must have prospered. Look at you now!"

"This is an illusion. I work for a company that buys and processes pineapples for export to the States. They want their management to look the part of success."

Just then the Colonel approached them. "Sir, may I have the pleasure of knowing with whom my companion keeps company?"

"Sir, my name is David O'Dea. I am with Higgins Pineapple Company."

"Yes, I am familiar with Higgins himself. He and I both graduated from West Point. In fact, I intend to invest in that company if the profit margin is acceptable. One of the factors that helps me decide on a good investment is the quality of the people that they hire. Tell me, did you serve in the war?"

David replied, "Yes, sir, I did."

"Did you engage the enemy?"

"Yes, I did at the Battle of Franklin."

"Oh yes, one of the best engagements of the war. Tore those sons of bitches apart, it did. That cripple Hood made every mistake that a field commander can make."

David did not reply but looked sternly at the Colonel.

"Whose company were you with?" the Colonel asked.

"I was on General Hood's staff," he replied.

The Colonel looked at him with immediate distain. "Bastard," he said softly and turned away.

THE COLONEL SPENT MUCH OF HIS TIME READING the telegrams that were relayed to the ship through international Morse code. He was anxious to know more about a possible impending conflict with Spain. War presented great economic possibilities to those who were willing to take risks. He pondered the financial implications should Cuba become a possession of the United States as he read the news.

Steel prices were bound to rise as heavy caliber artillery was being installed along the Texas coast for a possible invasion by the armies of Spain. In Galveston, concrete gun emplacements were already being built to accommodate the gun batteries.

"What about land investments in the Philippines?" he said to himself out loud as he scanned mentally the geographic holdings of the Spanish. Yes, victory held huge financial possibilities.

EVEN THOUGH THE COLONEL WAS OLDER NOW, a man in his early sixties, there was still time for him to be promoted to brigadier general. "Yes, possibilities," he reasoned. He felt that he was now in a position for good fortune to smile on him except for one thing, Ruby. "What if she had fallen over the side that dark foggy night? Damn it, the guests of the Captain were all staring at both of us."

THEN ONE MORNING THE ROLL OF THE SHIP CHANGED. Passengers began to crowd the starboard rail. Lookouts peered with binoculars towards the horizon. A small white cloud appeared faintly above the swells of the sea.

"Just a cloud," the Colonel assured Ruby authoritatively.

"Colonel, have you ever been wrong?" she asked sarcastically.

"Yes, one time and that was about you," he responded.

They remained silent as they looked at the small stationary cloud that seemed to simmer on the ocean swells. The chatter on the promenade deck increased in intensity. Soon an officer shouted down from the bridge to the assembly of first-class passengers, "Land to starboard!"

Ruby smiled towards the Colonel. "I guess this makes twice," she said with a smile.

SOON A PILOT BOAT APPROACHED THE SHIP as she neared Diamond Head. Once the pilot was taken aboard, two tugboats could be seen leaving Pearl Harbor. Their black coal-fed smoke billowed behind them in the stiffening wind. Their red stacks and gleaming white decks contrasted beautifully with the dark blue of the Pacific swells. Soon the color of the ocean changed from a dark blue to a lighter sandy green color that reflected not the depth of the ocean as some might have supposed, but the clouds above with their beautiful colors, like floating rainbows in the afternoon sun.

After the stevedores had moored the ship securely to the dock, the ship's company rang a bell that indicated that the passengers could disembark. As she neared the gangway, Ruby looked at the ship's officers in their stiff white uniforms with gold buttons. How handsome and young they were to her.

AS THEY PREPARED TO LEAVE THE SHIP, they were serenaded by Hawaiian women in grass-woven skirts accompanied by men playing ukuleles.

"The ancient volcano goddess Pele would not recognize the traditional dance performed in her honor," the Colonel said with disdain. "It is the image that we have conjectured in our own minds that the dance now honors." The air was perfumed by the sweet scent of flowers.

Two Chinese men approached the Colonel to carry down trunks of clothing and other essentials of travel in an unknown land. The small group in attendance followed Ruby and the Colonel as they descended the gangway and into an awaiting carriage for the trip to the Imperial Hotel that sat very close to the beach. It was a large wooden Victorian hotel filled with bright colors and woodcarvings. The wallpaper was a deep green hue that accentuated the dark woods used to create the exotic character of the hotel. An evening land breeze would soon carry the scent of orchids into the passageways of the hotel designed for the pleasure of the affluent.

Their accommodations consisted of two bedrooms joined by a common area that contained large cushioned wicker chairs and a mahogany desk that held a collection of the finest Cuban cigars. Large living plants grew in planters placed in the corners of the room.

The bedrooms were well apportioned. Above each highly carved bed was a canopy that also served to support the mosquito netting. Large open windows allowed the cooling trade wind into the room. From the open window, Ruby stood looking at the swimmers and those astride strange pieces of wood upon which they perched as they rode the waves to shore.

Once the house staff had unpacked their belongings and everything was placed in order, the Colonel looked at Ruby. "My dear, we do have a problem, don't we?" He did not wait for a response. "My wife is Catholic and will never agree to a divorce. You are pregnant and will not permit an abortion. We are, therefore, at an uncomfortable impasse. My friend has informed me that there is a steamer leaving for Ireland two days hence. She will round the Cape of Good Hope and will not require a Cape Horn Passage. I am willing to give you ten thousand in gold for you to return home and establish a new life."

"You bastard," she shouted, "what about your child? Think nothing of me. I will do one thing to avenge both the baby and me. I can assure you, I will name him Samuel Shell. He shall know who his father is and that he is a son of a bitch. When you die, he will be the heir to all your ill-gotten fortune, I swear. Since I expected you to abandon me and your unborn child, I have prepared a document that you must sign in order for me to leave without a scandal. After your death, the letter will testify that he is your son. Since you have no children and your wife is too old to bear you an heir, you have no reason to reject my offer."

"Like hell I will sign something! You want me to place my neck in a noose and then jump?"

"I like that analogy. I have not been sleeping at night like you supposed, but instead have been reading your papers and making notes. I know the routes of your spur lines and the politicians that you have bought. If you don't sign the paper, you will be ruined and in prison. That I can assure you. Don't think of having me vanish on this trip, I have written everything down. You see, I too have a lawyer whose identity is unknown to you. In the event that I die an untimely death, the circumstances of my death will be released not only to law enforcement but to all the leading newspapers and professional journals both here and abroad."

"Ruby, I seem to have underestimated you."

THE NEXT MORNING RUBY CHECKED OUT of their shared room and into a far smaller one. Upon her departure from the hotel, she ensured that her room costs were passed on to Colonel Shell.

The *Joyce* was a small steamer that transported passengers and freight bound for the city of Dublin. There was no grandeur about her. She was designed to carry a variety of cargo with passengers being only a secondary thought. Ruby did not mind for the ship's library contained both the classics and the pulp fiction of the era. She felt the growing child within her belly and was content.

She was happy to be finally going home. Her father had owned a mercantile store in Dublin. There would be enough money for them to survive. She kept the ten thousand in gold tightly sewn in the hem of her gown. She was willing to work hard and to do without, but her child, whether male or female, would receive an education that would ensure his or her good fortune in the world.

CHAPTER FOUR
The Return

"And the angel that talked with me came again, and waked me, as a man that is wakened out of his sleep."
                                        —Zechariah 4:1

SAMUEL SHELL III WAS BORN IN DUBLIN in 1897 to Ruby Smith Hamilton. Like his father, he was born on All Saint's Eve. After Samuel's birth, Ruby's mother fell ill with cancer. She died in the winter of 1898, a time of snow and bitter cold. Ruby remembered the banshee Badb Catha wailing loudly at the moment of her death.

Shortly after the birth of Samuel, just as the Colonel had predicted, the Spanish American War gripped the nation, and as consequence, the building of an even greater fortune for the Colonel occurred.

Ruby's family home would have been considered a row house, tall and narrow, except for being located outside the city of Dublin in close proximity to Montpelier Hill. Atop the roof were many flues designed to allow the peat smoke to escape. No matter how many fires were lit, the large tall-ceilinged rooms never seemed to warm. The slate roof reflected the frequent dark clouds that bore the heavy rains of Ireland.

She and her family lived in polite poverty. Her mother's family had once been members of the ascendancy, but now without land, they were simply members of Ireland's poor. Before leaving for America, her father had lost his fortune and much of their property through bouts of drunken gambling in which he played their assets against the cards.

Shortly after returning home, her sister went to Galway to live with a prosperous cousin, leaving Ruby and her young son to live in the large unattended to house filled with dark, damp rooms. Rooms that were filled with dust and the odor of decaying paper. Little sunlight found entry into the many chambers of the house.

The house stood alone on a small rural lane surrounded by large oaks and aged chestnut trees. There was a century-old yew tree that clung to life at the edge of the garden, its knurled wood and slowly dying branches hanging like arms over the unattended grass and wildflowers. Nearby were the ruins of abandoned stone huts and the remnants of a tower castle that was destroyed by the armies of Cromwell. A nearby field contained the remains of a cairn that at one time had held the graves of ancient peoples.

Samuel loved to play in a small fairy ring that resided in the large stonewall of the garden. Of particular interest to the young adolescent was the rising of the early moon over the garden's rough stone eastern wall. He was most content in the seclusion of moonlight when wild animals prowled and night birds sang in solitude.

The red front door of the house was faded by time and the frequent rains that formed over the Atlantic and quickly traveled across Ireland. The outside walls of the house were dark lichen-stained stone. The stones had been quarried from the valley head above Glendalough, the ancient site of an abbey. Two clear deep glacial lakes reflected the forest and mountains that surrounded the ancient religious site, the abbey cemetery filled with large Celtic crosses.

The windows of the house were shaded by large velvet drapes that reflected the Victorian era. The slate on the roof had been worn by time and had shifted allowing numerous leaks to occur in the upper rooms. On the frequently rainy nights in Ireland, the sound of dripping water could be heard as it struck the tin tubs that Ruby, like her mother before her, had spread out in the chambers.

Samuel would sit in his tall oak bed watching the raindrops form above him. A small lamp provided the illumination by which he read.

As a youth, he was much loved by his mother and felt a sense of privilege that was fostered by both his mother and the history of his family. He was told by his mother that his father was a wealthy American who had served as a colonel in the Union Army. He was also told that his father, a kind and generous man, had died in Hawaii. The ten thousand in gold was never mentioned to him.

Ruby invested the gold given to her by Colonel Shell in a lucrative Grafton Street fabric shop that sold cloth to be made into fashionable gowns worn by the wives of wealthy English landowners. The fabrics were imported from markets throughout the world including the Far East.

She had an uncanny business sense that was augmented by her great beauty. Before long, Ruby had a wealthy lover who lavished gifts upon her and her young son. Soon she had acquired a nearby jewelry store than specialized in the rarest of gems: the blue diamond.

Samuel was left to play with other young men of similar social status. He attended an exclusive Protestant school in Dublin. While popular with the students and staff, he remained aloof. He realized his role in the leadership of men despite his young age. His mother was an excellent model in the manipulation of others.

As a young man, he founded a secret organization that went by the Irish name, Club Thine Ifrinn. They held their meetings in a stone ruin on Montpelier Hill. The abandoned property had been the site of the notorious eighteenth century Hell Fire Club, a place of unholy rituals, purported sex orgies and drunken parties. It was a place rumored to have an association with Satan. The source of the rumor came from the allegation that the Club was built using the stones of an ancient cairn that had been the site of pagan burials.

One particular meeting of the club left a lifelong impression on the youthful Samuel. Its members had managed to steal liquor from their parents. Guinness and Jamison were carried in their leather school satchels to the ruin. There they built a fire in the great hall and began to drink. It was a stormy Friday night filled with the flashing of lightning and the percussion of thunder that echoed throughout the Wicklows. The children knew that their own parents would be out late and probably drinking a great deal of liquor themselves. The young boys planned to steal back through their bedroom windows. They would use the heavy, thick vines along the stone walls of their homes to gain access to their upper-story chambers.

There in the dim light of the dying fire, the young men, one by one, soon fell asleep. It was a fitful sleep as the great hall became colder in the chilled night air. Streaks of lightning could be seen touching the forest-clad mountains, their thunderous roars soon to follow.

To make rest more difficult, they were trying to sleep on the stone floor of the main hall using their book bags as pillows. As the fire began to die, smoke filled the room. Unable to fall asleep, Samuel leaned against a wall. He was finishing his drink when he noticed a movement in the far back corner of the immense room. A shadow of a person appeared standing in the entryway, indistinct in the haze of the dying wood smoke.

In a flash of lightning, he saw a woman wearing a torn full-length dress made of coarse fabric. Her hair was wet, moisture dripping from her hair and down her face. She was tall and very thin, almost athletic in appearance. The woman's skin was dark as seen in the vanishing firelight, her features sharp. As she moved towards Samuel, her footsteps created damp impressions on the dusty floor.

"Who are you?" Samuel asked, unsure whether she was real or only a figure in an intoxicated dream.

"I am Manuela," she replied.

"I do not know you," he said in a trembling voice.

"You are of my blood."

Then she backed into the entryway of the large stone room. The fire flickered and went out as a strong wind traveled throughout the room. Samuel remained trembling, pressed against the stone wall as his friends continued to sleep undisturbed.

The next morning, he awoke to the brilliance of the sun as it entered the empty window casements. The sunlight paused upon the stone floor for just a moment and then moved on. His friends awoke realizing that they should have been home much earlier. They knew they would be beaten with a cane or leather strap for sneaking out.

The children ran, leaving Samuel alone in the great vacant room. He expected the ghostlike figure to reappear. He felt unable to move from his position against the wall. Slowly, while trembling, he detached himself from the stone. He looked at the floor to see what size the foot impressions were but they were not there, only undisturbed dust covered the stone. At first, he walked, and then he too ran from the Hell Fire Club. He ran so fast through the sloping meadow that he tripped on a protruding stone. He fell upon soft clover and quickly regained his feet. He did not stop running until he entered the porch of his mother's house.

"Mother, Mother!" he shouted but no one answered. He ran from room to room looking for her. As he entered her bedroom, he looked beyond to the garden. Looking away from the house was a woman in a torn dress, her hair blowing in the wind. She had a wild, unkempt appearance. Sam froze in terror. He could not help but stare at her. She did not move.

Suddenly the woman turned, it was his mother smiling up at him. Her beautiful red hair pulled back, her dress the color of jade. "Samuel, Samuel, I missed you at breakfast. Where were you?"

Samuel did not respond but only continued to stare.

AT THE DINNER TABLE THAT EVENING his mother asked what troubled him. Earlier, he had retreated to his room. She was afraid he was becoming ill with a fever.

"Mother, I did something that will offend you."

"My Samuel, such a serious statement. I can't think of anything that you could have done that would bother or offend me," she replied.

"Mother, several of my friends and I spent the night at Montpelier. I know you told me not to go near the Hell Fire Club. I am very, very sorry I disobeyed you. I will never go there again."

"Samuel, you are trembling. What on earth scared you so? It is just an abandoned estate house that is in desperate need of repairs. I was afraid you might get hurt on the debris."

"No, Mother, the house is in remarkable condition except for the dust and animal nests that have collected in it."

"What then is to be feared?"

"I saw a woman there. I mean, I think that I saw a woman."

"I can assure you, Sam, that no woman would go near that house whether it be in the day or at night."

"But she did!" he cried.

"What did she look like? This imaginary woman?" Ruby asked.

"She was tall, slender and terribly unkempt. Almost wild in appearance. She looked wet all over even though it had stopped raining. It was as though she had fallen into a lake."

"Now Sam, it was only your imagination. I imagine you were asleep or had just awakened from a dream. Did she say anything to you?" his mother asked.

Sam stared at her intently. "She said that her name was Manuela."

"Sam!" his mother said firmly. "Where did you hear or read about Manuela? Did you read that in your father's diary?" The dairy was kept locked in the large walnut desk drawer.

"No, no," he pleaded.

"Yes, you have! I can't believe you would lie to me. The only mention of Manuela is in your father's diary."

"What diary are you talking about? You never mentioned that my father kept a diary."

"I took it from his briefcase when he decided to leave me in Hawaii. I thought there was another woman in his life besides his wife. In his dreams, he kept awakening and mentioning the name, Manuela. When I asked him who she was, he would only respond that he was dreaming. In his diary he mentioned her as only a recurring dream. I assumed it was some kind of childhood nightmare that had carried over into his adulthood. As far as I could tell, she was just an imaginary figure."

"You lied to me!" shouted Samuel. "You said my father died in Hawaii!"

"Your father is dead. He died several years ago."

"Why didn't you tell me?" asked Samuel as he fought back his anger and tears.

"You were so young. I wanted you to take pride in your family name."

"Where is my pride now?" pleaded Samuel.

"Samuel, what is important is that we have each other. Damn the rest of the world and their judgments." At that moment, Samuel understood the pain that his mother was experiencing. He walked over to her and put his arms around her waist pressing his body against her as a young child might do.

"Samuel, I don't want you to be like him. The only important thing that exists is to love and to be loved. Nothing more."

Samuel backed away from her. "What does that mean? What is love when it is built upon a lie?" He paused. "Who is she, the woman that I saw?"

"Samuel, I really do not know."

"Who can tell me what it means?" Samuel asked. "Do the dead speak?"

"There is a person on Grafton Street that has a gift. She conducts séances. I don't believe in such things, but it might be helpful to ask her. You know, people who are brilliant like W.B. Yeats, the poet, believe in such things."

GRAFTON STREET WAS FILLED WITH VENDORS AND SHOPPERS. A fiddler played loudly from the edge of the street, his violin case open for the tossing in of coins. The crowds, however, walked with a purpose not looking into the well-arranged glass windows of the various stores. Few lingered around for the afternoon wind was sharp.

Samuel and Ruby left Grafton Street and entered an alleyway that led to a dim cobblestone road lined with row houses. They walked briskly for the air was moist with the dampness of the sea. Large gulls cried from their perches on the buildings that were now darkening in the twilight. Samuel held his mother's hand tightly. He could not figure out why this was so important to his mother. He was the one who saw the spirit, not she. He expected her to be angry with him for spending the night in such a place. Instead, she seemed to be more interested in his father's diary. After all, he thought, it was just a name to her.

His mother stopped in front of a large house that stood on a corner, the house next to it having burned. Ruby took a small piece of paper from her skirt pocket and squinted at it in the dimming light.

"Yes, this must be the place," she said more to herself than to Samuel.

"Mother, how do you know this woman, this conductor of séances?" asked Samuel as he looked up at her.

"I don't know her, only of her. A friend said that a most unusual woman who could contact the dead lived at this address. She told me that Maud Meehan was born with a caul."

"What is a caul?" asked Samuel.

"It is a membrane that covers a newborn child's face. Very rare indeed. The midwife removes it and gives it to the mother as a valuable talisman. If the child becomes a medium, it gives her special power in contacting the dead."

"What relationship did my father truly have with Manuela? You reacted so strongly when I mentioned my seeing her. Now that I think of it, maybe I was asleep or just awakening from a dream."

"Yesterday I asked Father Joe about the happening. He said that it was just a child's imagination. He is probably right. What does it hurt, however, to have a little excitement, Samuel? After all, it will be an adventure for us to share. We both know that the dead are only asleep and that you and I cannot awaken them."

The breeze that blew down the unnamed street was very cold. Samuel just wanted to be by the peat fire and asked no more questions.

Ruby turned the knob of the large red door of the tenement house. Inside the odors of decay sought to escape from the opened threshold. The odors greeted them as though a vault had just been opened.

"Mother, I don't like this place. Please, let's go!"

"Hush, Samuel, if someone hears you, you will hurt their feelings. People cannot always choose where they live."

She took his hand and in a slightly tugging manner led him up the three flights of stairs to a landing that was lighted only by the skylight of the room. She knocked on the door. No one came. She knocked again, but only silence greeted her. As they turned to leave, Ruby heard someone gently walking towards the door. It opened.

"Can I help you?" asked a pleasant voice. Even though Ruby peered into the room, she could not see the person that had opened the door ever so slightly.

"I think you can," replied Ruby. "My friend Jennifer mentioned that you conducted séances. Is that correct?"

"I do not know your friend," replied the woman's voice.

"I am so sorry. Her friend, Mary O'Dea, mentioned you to her. I think that a gentleman hired you at the Grande Hotel to conduct such an séance about a year ago. Mary was in attendance at the time. Perhaps I have the address wrong. Is this 127 McGrath Street, Apartment 466? Of course, the streets are not well lit, and I may have misread the name of the street."

The faceless voice replied, "Yes, this is 127 McGrath Street. The apartment that you want is above this one. It is the only room at the top of the stairs. No one visits that room. I have never even heard a person walking up there. I always thought to myself that it was just an empty flat. I suppose I was wrong." The faceless voice gently closed the door. Ruby could hear the locks being re-engaged, and then the door was pulled on from the inside ensuring that it was indeed locked.

"Samuel, I guess that you and I are going to have to work for this one. One more flight of stairs to go."

"Mom, I saw only three stories on the outside, how can there be a fourth floor?" asked Samuel.

"From the street you can only see so far up. Sometimes they build rooms on the backside of the roof level. That way the wealthy that used to live in houses like this could have a garden area, well, sort of a garden area, for growing herbs and other small decorative plants."

Up the stairs they continued until they reached the uppermost landing in the building. As Ruby knocked on the door, it opened by itself as though it had never been closed.

"Hello, is anyone there?"

At her words, gaslights shot forth flames into the darkness of the room. The walls were covered in what appear to be a patterned red velour material.

Ruby and Samuel stood silently in the center of the room.

"Hello," Ruby said more loudly.

Then they saw her in the shadows of the great room seated at a large, dark circular wooden table with a solitary vessel upon it. No cloth covered the grain of the wood. Her hair was prepared in a fashionable manner. Her dress was off-white with pearl buttons. Her small-gloved hands rested upon the table, yet they appeared not to touch it.

Large mirrors on all four corners of the room presented a distortion of everything seen within.

"You may place fifty pounds into the urn," the beautiful young woman said.

Ruby was taken aback by the amount of money requested. She had withdrawn money earlier from the bank for other purchases but certainly not for what might turn out to be nothing more than a fraudulent act of showmanship. After hesitating, she counted the money carefully as she placed it into the silver urn.

"Now that you have paid, you expect something in return?" asked the woman.

What a strange question, Ruby thought. She then realized that it was simply a different way of asking her what she wanted.

"Yes, my husband used to awaken wet with sweat calling the name Manuela."

"That is not unusual for men who betray their wives and lovers to express a subconscious desire to be caught by those they betray. He may have been confessing to you in his dreams."

"Perhaps that might explain my husband's obsession with Manuela. I must admit, however, that I do not think that to be the case. He wrote about her in his private diary, not in romantic terms, but in expressions of dread. It was as though he was attempting to remove her from his thoughts but could not."

Ruby continued, "Then my son saw her, or at least he thought so, at an abandoned estate house where the members of the Hell Fire Club met a hundred or more years ago."

"Your son should never have gone there," replied the reader of cards.

"Yes, he knows that now," Ruby said as she looked down at Samuel who was still clutching her hand.

"I am sorry for that, Mother," Samuel said once more in an apologetic tone.

The medium looked at Ruby. "As you may know, the dead were contacted in the Old Testament, yet the practice is now forbidden by the Church. As a believer, why have you come to me?"

"I must know the truth. I know what the dreams did to my husband. They seemed to always be there even when he was awake. There were times when I thought he was talking aloud to someone that was not present. Now I see that this person has also entered my child's life. Can she be stopped before she becomes an obsession for him just as she was for my husband? Neither the Church nor a physician can help me. I thought that you might be able to rid my child's life of this spirit before it becomes a stronger force." Samuel was amazed at how concerned his mother was.

"Mrs. Hamilton, perhaps the spirit is not an evil one, but that of a person searching for someone who was lost. You were not his wife."

"How did you know my maiden name when I now go by Shell?"

"Do not ask a question that you are not prepared to know the answer to."

The gaslights flickered and then went out.

"Mom, Mom!" shouted Samuel.

"I am here," replied Ruby.

Just as quickly as they had been extinguished, the gaslights reappeared. The room was as it had been before, but the woman was gone.

"Hello, hello!" shouted Ruby yet only silence replied.

"Look, look, Mom!" said Samuel, his hands shaking. Where she had been seated, the chair was soaking wet, even dripping with water. The money was still in the silver vessel.

"Sam, take my hand! Do not look back!" Ruby said as she quickly led him from the room. Samuel was in front of her, holding onto the railing as there was not enough light to see the steps clearly beneath his feet. As they reached a lower floor, they ran down the remaining stairs and out onto the street. The chill, damp wind had been only a prelude to the rain that fell heavily upon them.

"Mother, you forgot to get the fifty pounds you left in the vase," said Samuel.

"No, it is now unholy money," she replied without offering further explanation.

SEVEN YEARS PASSED BEFORE SAMUEL SHELL entered Trinity College. As a student, he worked in the law office of Kevin O'Leary, Esq. One of his daily tasks was to scan the local newspapers for any event that might be of interest to the law firm. One day while drinking his tea, he noticed a brief notice regarding property located at 127 McGrath Street. The property was condemned after no buyer could be found. The condemnation proceedings had appeared in the venue of the court proceedings. After reading about the impending destruction of the property, he thought to himself that he would walk to McGrath Street and revisit the site of his and his mother's visit to the medium that night so long ago. Upon his arrival, he stood in front of the building and looked at the three stories. The windows were broken; the now faded outer red door was ajar.

Graffiti tattooed the outer walls. The large inner doors were still there just as he remembered them, yet they were unlocked, the locks having been stolen. In all probability, travelers had made the empty building a place of temporary lodging.

Samuel was very careful as he climbed the stairs that moved with each footstep. As he reached the third landing, he looked for the entryway to the top level.

There was no indication that there had ever been an additional floor to the building. The original wall and ceiling plaster were still intact. The wooden latticework above it did not indicate any disturbance in the three hundred years that the building had been on the site.

He opened the third floor door and peered into the chamber. Newspapers and discarded letters lay upon the decaying, rain-dampened floor. As he opened an additional door in the flat, a large bird screamed and flew through the missing window. He admitted to himself that many years had transpired since he and his mother had visited the medium, yet no rational explanation was forthcoming concerning the missing additional floor of 127 McGrath Street.

Could the medium have been the woman that he saw at the Hell Fire Club so long ago? "Of course not, of course not," he reasoned out loud to himself.

SHORTLY AFTER GRADUATING FROM TRINITY with a law degree, the new barrister decided to relocate to New York City. He did not want to become involved in the political turmoil descending upon Ireland. While sympathetic to the Irish cause, Samuel knew that revolution was not good for business. Even if Ireland was victorious in its struggle against centuries of British domination, he knew that it would take years to rebuild the infrastructure necessary for a vibrant economy.

In addition, he had many relatives in New York, some of whom had worked for his father. Their assistance might prove of great value to the ambitious young man.

CHAPTER FIVE
Well-Planned

THE GREAT DEPRESSION WAS JUST BEGINNING when Samuel Shell received word that his principal investment in New Guinea copper mines were falling short of predicted profitability. The great expectations fostered in the 1920s were now being torn from the spirit of the Wall Street investors. Fortunes that seemed so solid were now faltering, then suddenly crashing in value.

Even though Samuel now knew that his heavy investment in copper was doomed to lead to financial difficulties, he continued to convince himself that any raw commodity should in all likelihood bounce back as quickly as it had fallen. It became quickly apparent that his substantial investment would now yield only pennies on the dollar, if not liabilities. He also knew that few people truly understood commodity trading.

Slowly but surely a plan emerged, he would promote the idea of others investing in his copper mines. The first few buyers would enjoy a profit based on his selling of California land in the Long Beach area. He would, however, be careful to hold onto the mineral rights.

Promotion and timing would be everything. If a new investor was paid back a hefty sum on his investment in copper shares, the word would quickly spread throughout Wall Street. Other investors would arrive hoping to not only protect their wealth but to amass additional fortunes. With the new monies acquired, he would also pay the first few investors' handsome returns. The new investors would then have to wait their agreed upon term as the value of their shares hopefully increased.

The isolation of the Shell copper mines in the remote mountains of New Guinea would prevent inspections by the investors or their representatives. He would show the survey maps and legal documents establishing the legitimacy of their investments. He would need an accounting firm to provide financial records, one with a dubious reputation. Samuel would not publicly trade the shares since he feared that an additional layer of checks and balances might reveal the true value of the virtually worthless mines.

All Samuel had to do was wait for the Depression to come to a speedy end with the resultant rise in the value of copper. Events, however, would have to transpire with great precision.

It was already apparent that a new political star was rising in Germany. Such ambitions could lead to war. A war could generate a huge potential market for certain commodities especially copper. Not only would the investors be paid back with additional earnings, but he would have made a fortune as well. In the meantime, he would live, as he had grown used to, in great opulence.

Should an investor desire to cash in his investment, Samuel would simply show him a map with a new mine being located prominently on it ready to yield even greater returns on the money. New monies were then acquired from older investors.

He chose an accounting firm that had been struggling since the beginning of the Depression. An associate in Borneo would telegraph exaggerated earnings reports. Brooks and Sons Accounting Firm was an easy choice for Samuel since they had a reputation among a select few, including Mafia bosses, for keeping "loose" books.

Samuel knew that it was a calculated risk but worth the taking. He rented an office in upper Manhattan and had COPPER INVESTMENT, INC. written in bold letters across the glass front of the office. He placed his desk so that it ensured an excellent view of the East River for prospective clients to admire. The staging as well as a very attractive secretary were of great importance to any investor. Large survey maps of his holdings adorned the office wall. Everything appeared legitimate except for the profits derived from the four mines that he owned.

Fanciful documents that depicted an idyllic life in the South Pacific for the workers were used to describe in detail the profits to be made, including testimonials from those who had cashed in their chips due to a variety of providential misfortunes, often showing their smiling and thankful faces as Mr. Shell consoled them. Line and bar graphs demonstrated both the increasing value and the return on the dollar. The pages were also filled with abundant texts that further distorted the truth.

In the evenings, Samuel would sit at his desk looking at the East River far below him. Unlike other similar schemes, his worked in reverse order depending not upon a booming economy but one in which fear drove the business cycle. As long as he could ensure that his clients' investments were untouched over a substantial period of time, he was safe. The ratio of the inflow to outflow of cash was excellent, almost a business model for wise investment.

Just as he had expected, the young fanatical founder of the Nazi party rose quickly to domination. Copper was suddenly being demanded throughout the world as profits soared. What at first appeared to be a doomed strategy suddenly became an example of wise investment and brilliant planning. Even he was amazed that his clients did not lose money but indeed made new fortunes. His reputation as a financial wizard became well established on Wall Street.

He was more at ease than he had ever been. As he contemplated his increased fortune, he received geologic confirmation that an exceedingly large oil field lay just below the surface of the desert lands that he had acquired. The barren wasteland of the Los Angeles basin sat on a fortune.

Behind the planning and administration of the copper scheme was a young ambitious lawyer that he had met at an exclusive club in Manhattan. She was a graduate of Harvard Law. Orphaned at an early age, she was single and ambitious as she sought men of power and influence. Besides helping him foster his Ponzi scheme, she played the role of the attractive secretary when high-rolling investors were scheduled to pay Samuel a visit.

When they first met, he had poured out his frustration and anger to her. He was bored with his life and his wife. He needed someone to talk to, an understanding companion. Amber Joyce was just the kind of person he had been looking for. While she was too thin, her dark eyes captivated him. He had never seen such dark eyes in such a beautiful woman. She had the features of a woman from East Africa, perhaps Egyptian or Somali.

Usually Samuel was the kind of man who dominated a conversation, this time he chose to listen. She was the one who first mentioned the possibility of inflating the value of the copper mines.

"After all," Amber said, "they are thousands of miles away. With an adjustment to the production and earning sheets, you can offer the investors high returns on their money. By generating money from new clients, you can pay those that want to cash in."

Samuel did not trust Amber entirely for such beauty can be deceitful. He knew that success was his mistress, not a potentially fickle woman. She could turn on him at any moment if she so desired. She soon knew far too much about his financial dealings with the political elite of New York.

In 1946, Amber asked for an extended period of leave. For a year, she only wrote to Samuel. As time progressed, the letters became briefer. She had previously told him her mother was ill and she needed to care for her. Having been given shares in the mining companies, she was assured an income stream to support her financially.

When she returned to New York, she seemed very different to Samuel. At some point, she requested a larger share in the mining operation. Samuel did not know that she had given birth to his son who she placed in her mother's care. Amber did not love Samuel. Instead she feared that he would want to take her son away from her. She knew he would stop at nothing to get what he wanted.

One night when crossing the harbor aboard the Staten Island Ferry, she fell to her death in the frigid harbor waters. Some say they saw a man push her over the railing, others denied seeing anyone near her. The police report concluded that Amber Joyce had simply fallen over the railing. The reason for her death was unknown. Being unmarried and without influential relatives in the city, the matter was quickly closed.

Samuel did pay for the funeral. Present at the burial were Samuel and his attorney. No one else attended on that cold January afternoon, an afternoon of overcast sky and intermittent rain.

CHAPTER SIX

Dreams

THE DREAMS HAD NOT CEASED. With the end of the Depression and his newly gained wealth, he thought he could at last sleep soundly. Instead of feeling refreshed as demands to work late lessened, he felt ill at ease. When Amber took a year off from their projects, he fell in love with another woman, Roberta Webster. They got married just prior to the conclusion of World War II. His wife, the daughter of a prominent investor, reminded him that he was once more having terrible dreams that awakened her. It was as though he was panicked, like one who seeks to breathe but cannot.

"Samuel, let's take that trip we have been talking about. I would love to see Hawaii again now that the war has ended. We could stay at the Royale Hawaiian. Fort DeRussy is next door. I am sure that you will see some of your Boston College classmates on the beach. We could eat, drink and sleep as much as we want to."

After some additional prodding from his wife, they booked a flight. Soon they were flying on a Pan Am Clipper high above the Pacific Ocean. The roar of the engines produced a white noise that was conducive to rest. Even when he attempted to sleep on the flight, he had dreams that he could not recall when his wife, who was attempting to sleep next to him, awakened him.

She knew that they must be disturbing since he was covered in sweat. His wife told him that he was moaning loudly and kicking both his arms and feet as though he were swimming. When his wife asked him what he had been dreaming about, he was honest in his reply: "I don't know. I really don't." He began to dread and be afraid to go to bed because he knew the dream would resurface. Hoping not to enter REM sleep in which dreams are the most intense, he would light a cigar and prop himself up on multiple pillows.

"Sam, you have inherited the same problem your father had. Your grandmother told me about his dreams shortly before she died. He was tortured by them yet could not remember enough detail to discuss them with her. You have got to see a professional about this problem so that we both can finally get some rest."

Once they returned from the Islands, Sam inquired into who might be of help. He knew that a medical doctor would only be interested in prescribing drugs. He feared medication would result in putting him into an involuntary state of mind that he could not easily escape from. Instead, he preferred a generalist that he hoped would consider all aspects of his problem.

After much research, he entered the office of Dr. Steven Glass, Ph.D., a well-known expert in the field of oneirology. He had written a number of books that dealt with the scientific, philosophical and religious implications of dreams.

DR. GLASS LOOKED SERIOUS AS HE GAZED into the eyes of Samuel. "Tell me, why have you sought my help?"

The professor was a small, balding man who appeared to be in his mid-fifties. The austere nature of his office bothered Samuel who was much more familiar with opulent surroundings. It was apparent that the professor was more interested in his research than in the average client's mundane inability to sleep.

"Professor, I am bothered by recurring dreams in which I can only recall certain details. I do know that I awake sweating. My wife tells me that I react physically to the dreams. I think that my father and grandfather must have had similar dreams as well."

"How do you know that your father and grandfather had the same type of dreams?" the professor asked impatiently.

"My mother and my grandmother both told similar stories. The portions of the dreams that were most frequently mentioned to them were not prophetic, just strange in their consistency. In my dreams, a host of people surrounds something or someone on a beach. I cannot recall what the object in the center is. There is a strong feeling that a family is there, both past and present. Surrounding the circle is the sea, large swells rising and falling yet not touching those who are gathered.

"One woman in the circle that my father could recall was his Aunt Lilah. He told my mother that she was wearing a very large black hat that someone behind her kept tipping to one side. She would turn around, stare at the person and then face the object in the center of the circle again. The person behind her could not be identified. Aunt Lilah does not appear in my dreams or at least I don't think so. I had seen a very old photograph of her when she was in her thirties. The woman in my dream, however, is younger and far more attractive. She is very dark like someone who resides by the sea. She turns and looks away from me towards the large ocean swells. I can hear the waves breaking upon the rocks – my skin wet with their spray. This segment of the dream occurs over and over just as it did in my father's.

"Then I am swimming towards or away from the object in the center of the gathering. I do not know which.

"Suddenly I am standing in a very old rural Irish cemetery. I know that from the upright markers that are present. There are several very large Celtic crosses covered in a red lichen. Low clouds are racing past me and, judging by the clothes of those present, it is very cold. The men have their collars pulled up and the women are bundling themselves with heavy shawls. These portions of the dream are consistent with both my father's and my own versions of the dream.

"My father never mentioned anything about a song or singing. In my own dream, the people about the circle try to sing a church hymn but cannot start at the same time. For some strange reason, I, who can barely carry a tune, begin to lead all of those present in a different song. Oddly, I have never before heard the song that I sing in my own dreams. The name of the tune is 'When Shadows Fall.' I looked it up. It is a song from the 1930s. Nostalgic and all, nothing particularly spectacular about it. I really can't tell you why I know the words to it."

Dr. Glass leaned back in his chair, flicking the ash from his cigar into a metal waste can. "When a person mentions having a dream that is shared with someone else, it is because they have either discussed it beforehand, or it is an event that is well known to both parties. We often hear music transmitted through various media. We may not even be aware that we are listening, but our subconscious is.

"Dr. Sigmund Freud often contributed dreams to our deepest and most repressed desires and fears. The most common patterns represent the freeing of our obsessions that are visible only at the subconscious level.

"There are even some professors who suggest that dreams help prepare us for a threatening event that may take place in the future. It is the physical and psychological manifestation of the hyperactivity immediately necessary upon awakening that prepares us to combat whatever threatens us. In other words, the near constant REM movement experienced in deep sleep where dreams are born duplicates the consolidation of various sensory processes that never cease to interact with one another. This interaction is very necessary to survival, especially in a primitive state in which our evolutionary ancestors found themselves to be in.

"My preliminary assessment indicates that there is great fear within you as it was with your fathers before you, perhaps undefined in the conscious but present in the subconscious. When awake, you feel safe. However, when you're asleep, the subconscious removes the protective walls that separate you from your daily reality and that which lies deep, let us say, within the circle that you have described.

"There is little I can do for you once a dream has been established within the DNA. It is as much a part of your makeup as is the color of your hair and skin. In other words, it has now become an inherited trait. Probably several decades or centuries ago, something out of the ordinary must have occurred. So strong was the emotion that it became a physical part of you. If you have a son, he too will most likely experience a continuation of the dream. Let me restate my original hypothesis, there is no resolution to your problem.

"In the future, whether it be decades or centuries from now, the people will change, the clothing will change and so will the song, but the circle will remain."

CHAPTER SEVEN

Boston College

THE YEAR WAS 1991 AND SAMUEL SHELL VII was about to undergo a name change. He had been an ambitious student in high school. Samuel only cared about his own success regardless of its impact on other students. He would stop at nothing to be first in his class.

He was no longer called by his given first name, Samuel; instead his classmates had nicknamed him Maximillion due to his ambitious nature. Later his nickname became Maximilian due to the insistence of various computer spell checkers.

He was born to wealth, but found it boring. He found challenge in acquiring new fortunes. He lived to be even more successful than his forebears had been. The game was to start from nothing.

Maximilian did not manifest the typical foolishness of adolescence. Strong angular features and his tall height commanded the attention of all that met him. His thick black hair hung about his ears and neck, often unkempt. His deep brown eyes sought the inner mantel of anyone that he met.

He possessed a darker complexion than most of the other young men, a fact that he contributed to his penchant for sailing.

Young, ambitious and apparently from a well-bred heritage, he was quickly noticed by the debutantes in his various classes. Even though his major was business, he did take an Irish Studies class every now and then, in part due to his love of literature, but mainly so that he could be surrounded by either gifted or very wealthy young women. His sharp wit and renaissance personality commanded their immediate admiration. He could amend his conversation to fit the requirements of virtually any audience. Max was a champion of Trivial Pursuit.

His love for Irish Literature started when a young coed challenged him to read *Ulysses* – a book that was far from being popular on a Catholic campus but acknowledged by the faculty to be the greatest book of the twenty-first century. As proof that he had read the entire book, she promised to ask him questions. Together they were to later observe Bloomsday on June 16. The young lady was named Nancy Limerick.

Nancy, a shy, unassuming coed, was quietly attracted to him. At first, he did not notice her. Before she challenged him to read the masterpiece of James Joyce, she was simply a name in the roll call at the commencement of each class. He did notice the professors paying more attention to her. After passing her test on *Ulysses*, which assured her that he had indeed read the great classic, she agreed to see him occasionally. At this point in their relationship, they were only academically involved. He often sought her opinion on a variety of topics related to a book or poem that they were studying. To Max she was more than an average student, she was both gifted and observant.

Then one day in April she approached him in the hallway just outside their shared classroom. She asked him if he was lonely. At first he did not know how to reply to such an odd question. The last thing he wanted to admit was that he was not as popular as others assumed him to be. He had failed to develop any meaningful relationship with the more popular female students.

Max was in a classroom surrounded by beautiful young women, many of whom he had only exchanged glances with. He looked into the eyes of the unassuming woman who had presented such a unique question. "Yes," he responded.

She then handed him a yellow dandelion that she had picked on her way to class. She smiled broadly into his eyes. "I thought you might be lonely."

Max returned her smile. "May I have your phone number?"

She reached into her purse for a small slip of paper and wrote down the requested information. At first, Max could not believe that he had responded in such a fashion. That night he was restless in bed, tossing and turning, unable to sleep.

Who is this strange woman that wants to know me better? he thought. *It is one thing to share an academic interest but quite another to have a relationship.*

Late Sunday evening he called her number. Her roommate answered. He told her to ask Nancy if they might have a date on Wednesday evening. The Boston Pops were playing on the commons, and he thought that they might enjoy it. Her roommate told him that she would relay the message to Nancy.

Soon they were dating. Max managed to purchase an old wooden catboat with a snug forward cabin. The cabin was too small to stand in but perfect for sitting and sleeping. Soon their dates involved sailing around Boston Harbor at night. While cold outside, the small cabin and abundant wool blankets provided a protective environment for them.

"A bottle of fine red wine, soft music, fruit and a star-filled night. What more can I ask for?" he said to himself.

As the small boat rode the Atlantic swells that crept into the placid harbor, he proposed to her. After a moment's hesitation, she accepted. At that moment he placed a small diamond engagement ring on her finger. Their relationship had not lasted a full semester before they were engaged. They had both found the happiness that they had sought if even for a brief period of time.

In the fall, they had a traditional chapel wedding. A few friends, family and professors attended. Even though Nancy's family was wealthy even by Boston standards, she preferred to keep it intimate and private. Only those that she felt truly knew her were invited. Perhaps it was this meekness that attracted Max to her when so many others that he had dated wanted so much more than he was willing to offer as a self-supporting student.

Even though he came from a family with considerable holdings in oil, copper and utilities, he distanced himself from his own family. His success was to be his alone. Max shunned inherited wealth as though it brought a stigma to the holder of such assets.

AFTER ENTERING GRADUATE SCHOOL, he managed to get a job in a retail grocery store that specialized in exotic foods. As he grew to know his fellow employees, he found it somewhat alarming that nearly half of them had master's degrees from prestigious universities. They simple were unable to find meaningful employment. It became apparent to him that it was not enough to be brilliant or ambitious. Finally he admitted to himself that he needed the financial backing of a wealthy family. The more he thought about it, the more contented he became in his marriage to Nancy.

It was at this time in both of their lives that their love was the most unselfish. He wanted only to meet her needs and her, his. It was a love founded on the personality of the other. She was a lively conversationalist and excellent at proofreading his papers.

They moved into a small flat with neighbors above them. A

young Japanese couple lived beside them. Hachi and his wife Tami were quiet, scholarly individuals. They had a small, quiet son. Max loved to see them exiting their apartment since it gave him a chance to see the happy little boy. Those above them were seldom seen or heard. From their accents and appearance, he considered them to be Russian since they lived not far from an area of Russian-owned businesses.

MAX BEGAN TO CHANGE IN GRADUATE SCHOOL. He was no longer the humorous, cheerful person that had first attracted Nancy to him. Instead his mood became quite sober. In the evenings, he would sit silently staring out the windows at the top branches of the old oaks that lined Freedom Street. Nancy thought that he might simply be meditating or just trying to relax. Perhaps it was meditation since he was able to clear his mind of any dread while watching the metronomic motion of the tree limbs outside.

MAX WAS FOND OF SAYING, "'The business of business is business.'" He admired the directness of the quote that removed any consideration of the human element in business. He was generous to others simply because they often returned more than he gave.

He loved walking about the wooded campus, stopping to look at blooming flowers or the small lake that adjoined the college. But his ritual preoccupation was to visit a small art gallery not far from the campus. Many paintings of Ireland hung on the walls. One work of art, however, always commanded his attention. It was a painting of Benbulbin. Sometimes Nancy would tap his shoulder to remind him that it was time to leave the gallery. Even he wondered why he was so strongly attracted to the artwork.

FOLLOWING HIS GRADUATION, he used some of Nancy's inheritance to form a small investment company that soon prospered. Perhaps his timing was great or his business acumen was highly refined. He had learned early to surround himself with the most competent people possible. Max knew that he was in an excellent location to find the talent needed since Boston College, Harvard and MIT were in very close proximity.

He preferred to hire Boston College graduates since he was Roman Catholic. The college had been founded as a Jesuit school for the Irish that Harvard had shunned. Regardless, he had a talent for seeking out the most gifted of applicants. He did not concentrate on grades, personality or looks but on drive. How desperate was the applicant to succeed and, therefore by default, to serve him? He also knew that his family fortune was available if it was ever needed, an insurance policy against failure.

Soon he had enough money to move into real estate and with it the construction of small shopping malls. It was at this point that he realized that if he was to succeed further, he had to remove the human element of compassion from the workplace. Only the job had to matter to him and nothing more. He felt that it was necessary to be considerate of his employees if only to make them more productive.

His work hours became excessive and increasingly he was away from home. It was not long until a child was born. He felt that the baby was Nancy's idea and not his. He did not have the time for a child when he was building a financial empire for himself. He preferred to move in the circles of the wealthy. Yet, he never felt that he belonged to the country club sect. Outwardly, he would say his family was most important to him, but everyone close to him knew it was not true.

Nancy did not need him to garner more wealth in order for

her and their son to be happy. It was at this point in their marriage that Max began to relish even more control over others around him. From the custodial service employee to one of his vice-presidents, he was the boss. His specialty, at least to others, was the one-way conversation. To Nancy, he was increasingly becoming a stranger. He often told her that she did not love him enough. Meals were never nutritious enough. Max often read the health section offered by a variety of media. He would then accuse Nancy of not providing the correct environment related to food and cleanliness. If one source said that more vitamins were necessary for health, he would accuse her of not providing enough. When he read that vitamins were harmful, Max accused her of giving him too many vitamins.

His young son bore the brunt of his criticism and became the surrogate for his wife. He would often shout at the infant, threatening to strike him with his fist. If the small child made a mistake, it was her fault for failing to teach him. If he cried, she had made him weak. The young boy could hear the arguments that originated often in the kitchen.

Max's discontent carried over into all facets of their home life where he continued his work late into the night. His evenings were filled with computer screens, texts and phone calls. The only company they had was his employees and potential business partners. There soon was little conversation between Nancy and Max, only what to some observers appeared to be orders related to mundane household chores. In the quiet background, a small silent child played alone.

CHAPTER EIGHT
Holbrook House, Ireland

The Familiar

I have loved you far too long.
Daily chatter no longer heard.
Mundane habits to endure.

A song sung to those that do not listen.
The seasons change, as do our lives.
Hollow words of love are spoken to those that do not hear.

THE MIST WALKED SOFTLY FROM OFF the distant cold ocean, its breath touching the stones of Holbrook estate. Moisture dropped to the pebbled drive off the eaves of the Edwardian estate house, a pretentious six-bay house of slate-colored stone. Within the protective windowpanes and lead-encased stained glass, a fire shot forth flames in the large stone hearth.

Why they had purchased Holbrook was a question that neither Max nor his wife Nancy could answer. After buying the estate, he often referred to it as "her house, her dream."

At this point in their marriage, they had traveled only one time to the coast of Connemara for a short visit to see his elderly grandmother who returned late in life to the small coastal village of Cleggan. His conscience bothered him in that he chose not to visit her during the pursuit of his career. Max knew he should have spent more time with her during her lengthy illness, but instead chose to open a suburban mall near Rockwall, Texas. Upon receiving word of her death, he paused only a moment before returning to the task at hand – that of accumulating more wealth and power.

For a short period of time, he contemplated going back to Ireland since friends and relatives expected it of him. Max believed, however, that he did not have the time to travel to Ireland for the funeral. He quoted a paraphrase to himself from the New Testament, "'Let the dead bury the dead.'" He felt that she would understand, but he inwardly knew better. There was no time to worry about things that he could not change.

After the mall was constructed and sold to Chinese investors, he had an odd desire to return to Ireland to visit her grave and see relatives that he had not thought of in years. He could not, however, fully understand why he decided to return to Ireland, a country that he had previously ignored. It was true that Max's father was of Irish descent. Max himself was born in Boston.

After the divorce of his mother's grandparents, Max's grandmother had returned to Ireland in order to be near her relatives.

Mary Cunningham loved Ireland with a great passion. No matter how much Samuel Shell had tried to persuade her to return to the States, she refused. She was a strong-willed woman with a code of rigid discipline.

Later, Max often thought that while she was too harsh on them as kids, she did teach them the value of money and hard work.

Mary had been a devote Catholic and insisted that her children be the same. They obeyed her without question for to do so otherwise would have resulted in the intervention of Father Joe who was a proponent of corporal punishment. He believed firmly in King Solomon's advice: "Spare the rod and spoil the children."

Max knew that Mary loved the scriptures, especially the King James Bible which was her favorite translation. She was fond of quoting from the Song of Solomon:

> I am *black, but comely, O ye daughters of Jerusalem, as the tents of Kedar, as the curtains of Solomon.*
> Look not upon me, because I am *black, because the sun hath looked upon me...*
>
> By night on my bed I sought him whom my soul loveth: I sought him, but I found him not.

When older, he finally developed the courage to ask her why she would only quote two passages when the rest of the Song of Solomon was so beautiful in its entirety. Her answer had always bothered him.

"Max, you have olive-colored skin, dark brown eyes and raven-black hair – have you ever wondered why?"

Max replied, "Oh, I guess that is why some of us are called Black Irish."

"Max, think deeper. The peoples of North Africa once invaded Spain and portions of France and their bloodlines were carried throughout all of Europe, perhaps even to Ireland. You may carry some of their genes just as I imagine that your grandfather did. He was dark like you. He would never, however, admit it. He always blamed the sun for his skin color just as the lover did in the Song of Solomon."

Mary continued, "There were stories told within his family about a far distant relative who loved a Moorish princess. Your father thought of them as only fables, old wives tales, but I think there was some truth in them."

UPON HER DEATH, HIS GRANDMOTHER WAS BURIED in the small graveyard that surrounded Drumcliff Church, famous as the burial site of renowned Irish poet W. B. Yeats. Various great-aunts and great-uncles wrote to Max pleading him to visit her during the months preceding her death. He chose to ignore them, failing to respond to their pleas.

"Who are they to tell me how to spend my time?" he shouted to a friend while having a bourbon and coke at O'Casey's on the east side of New York's financial district. "I tell you who they are, they are nobodies. Poor destitute bastards that have chosen to sit on their Irish asses rather than leave Cleggan and amount to something. They must have heard that I have money. That drives men to give advice, especially to relatives." After a brief pause, he continued, "Share, share, like the Devil I will."

Yet now he felt the need to return to that which was so familiar to him. His dreams laid the foundation for his awakened thoughts. He longed for the Irish craic and the companionship of his youth. Something about Ireland would not let him go. His grandmother had little money when she returned to Cleggan, his grandfather had seen to that.

As a teenager, Max was sent to live with his grandmother in Ireland. His father felt that this should be a learning experience for him and did not provide the youthful Max with sufficient funds on which to live the life that he had been accustomed to. The short visit was, however, to last four years since no return ticket had been provided to him. He would have to earn his passage home.

Max found work on the ferry that connected Inishbofin to the small village. As a line handler, he also assisted the passengers in boarding. He remembered all the American tourists with their expensive luggage and condescending attitudes.

Max wanted to have someone carry his luggage and address him as "sir". Yet the work on the ferry and, later on, a small trawler toughened him as his father had intended and created a love for the sea that would not pass from him. His hard work taught him the value of every coin that he earned.

His grandmother often told him about a far distant relative that had been made a slave of the English and forced to journey to Barbados. The stories about him fascinated Max as a youth. That distant relative's vow to return to Ireland and revenge his family was always a popular myth with Max and his friends.

Whether these stories were true or not did not bother him. They were told over and over again in the pubs where details were added with each retelling of the story. Craic, a good yarn and a Guinness summed up his memories of Ireland, that is, the part that he chose to remember.

He did not want to visit his father's distant relatives who had moved to England for that country held only bitter thoughts, feelings that were only intuitive and not based on actual experience. The fussing of his parents, the blows to his buttocks even as a teenager. The constant reminders of his lack of faith in the Church. His disrespect to his teacher and the impoverished vicar, who was forced to moonlight as an instructor, always resulted in harsh beatings.

Why should he, Max reasoned, remember everything he hated so much in youth, yet in spite of himself, could not forget? "There is enough pain without searching for it," he often said to himself. He knew that memories would appear whether he invited them or not, especially at night when the house was quiet and memories were all that he possessed.

THE YEARS HAD PASSED VERY QUICKLY since the childhood visit to his grandmother. On the day of his return to Ireland, it rained heavily. As he stepped from the airplane at the Shannon Airport, he breathed deeply the wet, sea-scented air. A gale created by the death of a hurricane sent heavy rains sweeping onto the coast. Black clouds hung low over the distant salt-rimmed swells of the open sea.

He rented a car at the airport. Unaccustomed to the small SUV, he hit the side view mirror against a waste container while leaving the airport. He got out of the car and shouted, "Why the hell do they still force you to drive on the wrong side of the road? Why can't they be more American since there are more Irishmen in the United States than there are here? If the steering wheel had been placed on the left side of the car where it belongs, I would not have hit it against the shit can!" He did not want to waste time explaining the scratch marks on the mirror's pedestal to the rental agency.

THE TIME SPENT REACHING THE COASTLINE OF CONNEMARA was

brief since Ireland's introduction of the modern expressway – not like the long trips that he remembered taking with his grandmother. As he approached Drumcliff, sadness fell upon him as the clouds struck the rim of the nearby sacred mountain. Max got out of the rented car, his black woolen coat shedding copious amounts of water. Nancy waited in the rental vehicle for him as he searched for his grandmother's grave. After locating it among the ancient stones, he knelt down and said a silent prayer. The wet grass felt cold on his knees. Wild birds flocked to the trees while sheep bayed in the nearby meadow. There in the distance was Benbulbin, the ancient mountain that reached towards the sea, sunlight chasing clouds upon its slopes.

HAVING RENTED A NEARBY ESTATE HOUSE not far from Donegal, he and Nancy soon fell in love with its ornate rooms, walled gardens, fruit trees and the sensual nature of the house. A house built of stone appealed to him in so many ways. Max would walk along the beach at low tide. From there he would admire the house that was built in the eighteenth century. It represented strength that endures. In particular, he enjoyed that its walls bore the green damp moss.

SOON HE MADE AN OFFER TO BUY THE ESTATE. He did not wish to bargain but instead offered a generous amount to the owner who was more than happy to accept it. Property values had rapidly descended since the earlier building boom when other Europeans and Americans had gleefully invested large sums of money in the speculative market of natural beauty and nostalgia. Perhaps the decision to purchase the house was his atonement to Nancy for a marriage where actions no longer conveyed the poetic verse of a shared love.

People often said to Nancy, "If he was having a midlife crisis, wouldn't it have been cheaper for him to buy a red Ferrari?" Then too often the statement was followed by the comment, "My husband says that a major purchase at his stage of life usually occurs when there's an affair in the midst. You know, one of those office things."

NANCY PLACED HER BLOODY MARY on the round teak coffee table.

"Why do people fall in and out of love? What draws two strangers together to bond in such an intimate way? Is it frailty or strength that unites them only to later let go?" Nancy asked her friend Margaret, whose eyes rested upon an unread tabletop book, a pictorial journey through the Louvre. Margaret had just recently flown to Shannon from New York. Her husband John and Max were business partners and shared a mutual love for golf. Located nearby was a golf course well known for its fairways and beautiful views of the sea.

Margaret was a nervous, small-framed woman. When she was seated, her crossed legs were in constant motion. About her was a continuous cloud of cigarette smoke. Even though she had survived, despite the odds, breast cancer for ten years, a cancer found in 11 out of 17 nodes, she was determined not to alter her lifestyle. Margaret felt that if she altered any variable in her hectic life, she would surely die of the disease. She also felt that if she slowed down her daily routine that her life would be shortened.

Margaret's time was filled with charity works, shopping and visiting her friends. She made it a habit to eat out every day with a different person. Margaret looked up at Nancy. "Well, all I can give you is an opinion tainted by my own personal experience. The letting go of love follows an affair. For my John, it was an affair with a waitress that he met at a Cracker Barrel. It was a long time ago, back when Max and John were just starting out in the oil business. You remember Gulf Coast oil was where the money was at that time. The malls and more business trips came later on."

"Can you believe that about the waitress? He was busy on his Blackberry texting friends back at the office when a waitress approached him. You know the type, dyed blond forty something slut. He had just ordered the Sunrise Sampler, better known as the carotid artery special, when she said, 'Throw that damn thing in the lake and let's go to PC.'"

Nancy looked at Margaret somewhat puzzled. "What is PC?"

"Oh, I forget that you never had a husband stationed in the South. PC is Panama City. It is a small coastal town in LA."

"LA?"

"Oh, sorry again, I mean lower Alabama."

Nancy could not help but laugh. "You mean your John, the straight-laced John that I have known for so many years, had an affair with an interstate waitress? I thought he was a deacon in your church. It just shows how untrustworthy men can be." She paused. "How long did it last?"

"Long enough for me to find out about it. Do you think that anything remains a secret? That fool later bought her an expensive ring. Well, as you can imagine, the bank called asking about the purchase. Men can be such fools. They think they can outsmart a woman, but they can't," said Margaret with a high degree of confidence.

"But you divorced him and then went back to him," stated Nancy. "Until now I never knew why you divorced him."

"Are you kidding? I stay with him just to make his life miserable. That is my purpose in life. Besides, I am now his common-law wife. I can stick it to him anytime I please."

Nancy looked at Margaret. After a brief pause, she said, "I can only suspect what happened between Max and me. As you know we never talk about our son that died so tragically. It is as though we have divorced his drowning from our thoughts, like he never really existed. I don't think that the wound will ever truly heal. He will not admit it, but I think that he still visits Aran in his dreams." Margaret did not ask her to relive the death of her son for she knew that it was too painful.

Nancy continued, "We grew further apart after he sold his interest in suburban malls. His company constructed them during the late building boom in Dallas. He was smart to sell the properties just before the bottom of the market fell out. Max is a man with great confidence in himself but too often feels disdain for others whom he just naturally assumes are less gifted then he is. My Max is fond of saying, 'Are there really any gifts? We all will eventually sit silent in a room regardless of our talent. It is just a matter of time. Age, dementia, Alzheimer's – they are all the same thing. They are the masks that we must eventually wear. It is better to be the King's jester than the King since we who have obtained so much must eventually experience such an abysmal fall.' He is also found of quoting his grandfather, or is it his great-grandfather, heaven only knows: 'Old age is like being drunk without pleasure – you forget, stumble and then fall.' It is obvious that he comes from a long line of pessimists. They also had another thing in common: they were all tormented by dreams."

After sipping from her drink, Margaret said, "Nancy, tell me why you call him Maximillion?"

Nancy replied, "I think that the name Maximillion is better suited to a man who thinks only of money and not of those who helped his ascension to the throne of what he now considers as hell."

"What on earth are you talking about?" asked Margaret.

"He now equates money with failure. Can you believe that asshole? I think that he even blames me for his success. Just the other day he said that he wished he had become an Irish monk and lived on the Hebrides, those remote islands off the coast of Dingle. He wouldn't have lasted a day there unless there was both Scotch and a whore nearby."

"Nancy, you are really making me concerned. I have never heard you talk about him like this before."

"I never had reason to until now, and I thought that confession was good for the soul. What a crock of shit!"

"You really don't know what you are saying. Have you failed to take your Valium? Few people have been as fortunate as you and Max – with houses on two continents and a condominium in Hawaii. I can't believe you are serious when you fault him."

"You just don't know," said Nancy as tears trickled to her blouse, dampening a simple gold cross that she had worn since her father had given it to her in Boston when she was but a child. She touched the moist cross. "This is the only thing that is truly mine that has lasted. He will eventually treat me the way his grandfather treated poor Mary, his grandmother."

"Nancy, I think that I had better prepare you another Blood Mary. Come on, you are not too old, and Max is a very loving and extremely successful man. Many women would love to be with him including John's fucking waitress friend. Most of us are married to borderline creeps. You know the kind, they live only to fuck and shout during the Northeast Conference games."

"Well, Margaret, I thought that you and John had the perfect relationship. Two people on a second trip around, not remarrying to avoid further divisions of estates and yet madly in love. I never thought about the common-law aspect of your relationship. I will have to keep that in mind should Max and I ever divorce." Nancy paused. "Max and I often sat on the balcony of our condo watching you two frolicking in the warm Pacific waters with no care in the world."

"Nancy, a mai tai must have affected your vision. You probably saw two people fussing just before a real fight. Sort of like knights jousting for a position before one or the other kills his opponent," said Margaret with intensity as she lit another cigarette, her smoke drifting towards the large fireplace like a finger pointed towards a window. "Don't you have anything to go with this drink, you know, like Adapin or some shit like that?"

"Margaret, be careful with what you mix together. I don't think that your ninety pounds can handle a great many drug interactions. How in the world did you lose so much weight?"

"No secret there, a lap band and speed."

"Yet you stay with him, and you two are not even married."

"Despite what I said earlier, I really don't know why I love him, I just do. Habit? The desire for self-punishment?" Margaret turned her gaze towards a picture of the four of them with a Kentucky derby winner in the background. Their smiles frozen in the black-and-white photograph. Contented, happy, yet each alone. Both women knew that they had become actors in their own plays.

THE WIND BROUGHT RAIN FROM OFF THE ATLANTIC. The rain pounded on the windows, then bounced to the stone below. The room where they sat became cold. The house with its large, drape-shrouded windows smelled of decay – that rich aroma of wealth where love is not found. Nancy knew that it was not long ago when Irish roses filled the rooms with sweet scents and gardenias blossomed in the extensive gardens kept safe behind the large protective stone walls.

Max had married Nancy for only one reason, he loved her. Later he stayed with her because her father was the chairman of an East Coast corporation that specialized in the manufacture and distribution of parts for exotic automobiles. It was true that Nancy was a very attractive and educated person. The tennis pro had made several attempts to allure her with his talents. She merely thought his efforts to be immature. He felt he was entitled to flirt in his position as senior tennis instructor. What else in life did he possess other than his tan and dark black hair? Only to herself would she admit her attraction to him. In many ways, she needed his attention. Like a reassurance that she was of value even if it were only for sex.

Nancy was a quiet woman that immersed herself in various liberal causes much to Maximilian's displeasure.

"If you give to a charity, they will put both of us on their damn call and mailing lists! Nancy, haven't you learned anything in life? You are too damn innocent! Too easy to fool. Never ever help the enemy and, in case you don't know, the poor are our enemy. Why do you think the great estate houses are but roofless ruins? The damn poor burned them, that's why!"

How can I argue with only an opinion? Nancy thought. *I could appeal to facts, but that would be useless, too. Facts do not matter in a solar system in which my husband is the burning star.*

THAT NIGHT NANCY LAY AWAKE in her four-poster mahogany bed listening to the sounds of the ocean and of the house itself. She could hear the popping sound of the logs coming from the main fireplace. The peat fire in her bedroom burned silently. She did not want to mention to Max that she had earlier found a lump in her breast. That night all of her rationalization regarding the small growth fled from her. The stark reality that it might be cancer came vividly to mind as she tossed alone in her bed. She thought about her own mother's battle with breast cancer. She sensed that even though they had access to the best doctors, her battle with the disease could only end in death. She no longer had the will to survive, and she inwardly knew that would be the greatest impediment to living.

Max slept in a smaller bedroom down the hall on the opposite wing of the seven-bay house. After a warm bath, he dressed in his high-buttoned pajamas. He walked barefoot to the tall bed that required a small stepladder to climb upon. There he felt the soft pillow, covered himself with many blankets and soon fell asleep. Quickly he saw the ocean with rising swells. Its water was a deep blue except for the crests of the waves that were a transparent green. The top of each swell was coated in white frothy foam. He knew that the swells were rising in the Caribbean Sea, an ocean that he had voyaged upon on many occasions. The cruise line that he preferred often left from Fort Lauderdale, a small line with outside, expensive cabins. Other times they would fly to the West Indies. There they would stay at a seaside villa. As the wind awoke with the morning sun, Max would set sail in one of the many small day sailers that lined the harbors of the various islands. Nancy often wondered why he did not charter larger vessels since he was very capable of crewing a larger boat. To her question, he would reply, "There is no one here to impress, only myself." He never felt better than when his hand was on a wooden tiller or on the spoke of a nautical wheel.

In his dream, the swells rose and fell in a repetitive fashion. On the far horizon was a solid line of black clouds moving swiftly towards him. He was aboard a small sloop. Its sails were straining in the wind that blew from abaft her beam. His fist was locked on the small tiller. Then suddenly, a hand covered his. A tender hand, that of a stranger. Her skin was dark like those in the shrines that he had visited in India. No, far darker. He could not see her face, only her form in the wind-flung spume. Max knew that whoever this stranger was, he loved her.

Then he saw himself walking along the beach. There before him was the small skiff. Its sails were blown out and its wooden hull open at the seams as small crabs ran in and out of it. He felt a great sadness as he touched the decaying wood. The ocean about his feet was cold, not like that of a tropic sea. Overhead, the clouds swirled and raced towards distant tropical peaks, the pitons of an island not known to him.

Max suddenly awoke. Outside he could hear the crashing surf and the moaning of the wind that sought entrance into his room. His body was covered in hot sweat like that of a person in a panic attack.

"What kind of a dream was I having?" he muttered quietly to himself, having forgotten the repetitive nature of his inherited dream cycle. "It's the sound of the ocean just outside my window that has caused me to think of the sea. That's all."

Max arose and looked out his window. The sea was very still; only a faint whisper of the surf was heard. The stars shone brightly as though it were the moment of creation. In the distance, the faint glow of a lantern could be seen moving with the fluidity of a person's gait. "What fool would be up at this hour on the beach? Must be an old man who can't sleep. If he has a wife, she is probably like Nancy."

AT BREAKFAST HE STILL FELT BOTHERED BY THE DREAM. He looked towards his wife. "Nancy, I think that I will go into Sligo and visit a pub that a cousin of mine used to own. No telling who I will see there, maybe even one of my damn relatives. I may stop by Drumcliff on the way back, so don't expect me to return at any given time."

Nancy looked at him knowing that her desires for the day would only be secondary to his. "As you wish," she said sadly while looking out the window towards the garden where rose bushes were aflame in brilliant and varied hues. A small songbird alit upon a branch of a pear tree and began its beautiful yet haunting song. She knew that she would spend the day once more alone in a great house far from her family and friends. She ached for those that she loved but could not be near.

Later in the hour, she heard the Mercedes crank. She peered out the window as the car drove down the pebble driveway. As it entered the main highway that led to Sligo, she continued staring and felt a deep emptiness within herself.

As Max drove, he thought about his grandmother and the marvelous stories that she told him about her youth in Ireland. She loved W. B. Yeats and his mystical poetry. She was even invited to visit Coole Park, the estate of the late Lady Gregory. She often would ask Max what Yeats meant by the words on his gravestone:

Cast a cold Eye
On Life, on Death.
Horseman, pass by!

Max could have gone to the library and found a scholarly interpretation to what the great poet had written, but instead he enjoyed pondering various meanings. His grandmother never shared with him what she thought was the bard's intention.

"Life and death are the same," he said to himself. "No, that is not it. The Horseman is always betrayed as death. The poet did not want to die, yes, that is it. Poor chap, couldn't change his destiny even with the Noble Prize. We fools come to stare at his marble, nothing more. Oh well, maybe to ponder what is written upon it. Like all of his works, I never could understand a damn thing that he wrote. I think he was almost as confused as was his fellow Irishman, James Joyce. Then you have Picasso and Salvador Dalí. Only idiocy is recognized as having merit in the fine arts."

IN THE LIGHT RAIN THAT DAY Max peered down at the stone of Yeats. "Perhaps the meaning is unique to each of us who reads his words. Lack of clarity leads to inner searching and, thereby, we join the poet in his words or some shit like that."

At his grandmother's grave, he stood but for just a moment. "Grandmother, I wish that you could hug me today. I want to feel the comfort of your breast against my cheek. To hear you say, 'It will be okay, I promise that it will be.' Who comforts me now? Not stone or the words of a poet. Perhaps there is no comfort. That is what lovers are for. I only wish I knew."

As he left Drumcliff, a small tear ran down his cheek. The man who could fire dozens without remorse now wept on a rain-slick highway that led to Sligo and a pub that he only faintly remembered.

THE WITCH'S TEAR WAS A SMALL TAVERN located on a side street in the sea-nourished town of Sligo. Everywhere that a person drove or walked, the scent of the sea was present. He parked his car and stared at the entryway to the pub. It was as he remembered it – cold and green-tinted by the moss that dwelt upon its surface. The window frames were covered with delicate decay and flaked paint. Even the GUINNESS sign was faded for there was no reason for that company to invest in a small pub that, like a church, was only frequented by old and soon-to-be-dead customers.

As he entered, there were several men seated at a table. One raised his pint and toasted the unknown visitor. "Slàinte mhath! Good health to you, a stranger in our midst."

Max remembered his Irish. "Slàinte mhath to all present."

He walked over to a dimly lit table where the only source of light was from the cloudy windowpanes that rose to the height of the ceiling. Dark wood added to the dimness of the pub and accented its age. Scents of liquor, pipes and cigarettes served him as faithfully as the proprietor.

"What will you have? A pint of Guinness and soda bread?"

"Yes, and some of your oyster stew," Max said.

"Now how did a Yank know about my oyster stew? I have to admit you seem somewhat familiar to me. Of course, you must have some Irish blood in you. No strangers come to this part of town."

"My name is Samuel Shell. My mother was an O'Flaherty."

"I be damned and bless the saints," said Thomas O'Malley, "if it isn't Samuel all grown up. Damn, it has been a long time. I suppose that you want to see your cousin Denis. Well, I hate to tell you this, but he died several years ago. I married his sister and, bless her soul and all the saints of Ireland, she is buried not too far from your grandmother's grave. Damn, it is you, Samuel. I remember all the trouble that you and me and all the rest of St. Joseph's school got into that night when we had a beer party up on the cairn. You know that was a holy place to the believer. Yeah, you and I hauled the beer kegs on our backs up Knocknarea and planted them right on top of Queen Maeve's Tomb. If you had not built a fire, no one would have known we were up there. I remember the horror on your face when you saw Father Joe approaching us. The whole town knew what we were up to. Shit, they could see the whole thing from the streets of Sligo. Damn, those were good times even though I had a hard time sitting down after Father Joe laid the rod of penitence to my butt."

"You know, I think Father Joe was only mad because he fell down several times trying to climb that damn mountain in the dark. Otherwise he would have enjoyed a good drink with us," said Max.

"Like hell. He was a bastard then and still is. Do you

remember when we stole the skiff down at Sullivan's and sailed her over to Inis Airc?" said Thomas, laughing.

"There are some things that are best not to remember," Max said quietly, almost confidentially. Max could feel the stare of a person yet he could not see him. He turned around on the bar stool. In the far shadows of the bar, he could see the outline of a man sitting alone. In that the restroom was in the direction of the person, he rose and walked towards him.

"Excuse me," said the man who appeared very old, yet still curious. "I remember your grandmother. She and I used to talk a great deal about you. Shame you did not visit her when she was dying."

"I must admit that I have made some bad choices," said Max as he looked deeply into the eyes of the stranger. The stranger's face was wrinkled like that of a seaman. Both sun and wind had increased the depth of the furrows about his brow. As he spoke, he grasped at the air that he breathed, each breath a struggle to claw at that which is sought but cannot be had. His woolen cap sat awkwardly on the crown of his head. His coat was that of Irish tweed, the sleeves frayed and the elbow patches well worn.

"My name is O'Sullivan. Seems to me like you have not found what you are looking for. Typical of Americans who think that they can buy just about everything, yet at the end of their lives possess nothing. Not even that which was free to them at the very beginning of their search. They never knew the worth of their own mother's milk."

"Well, I assume then that you have it all. I have never yet met a philosopher that had the money to pay for his own pint."

"True, but what I own is enough to satisfy me."

"What might that be that has such value?" asked Max irreverently.

"Knowledge about events past and yet to be."

"That must be of great value, like owning the wind," replied Max sarcastically.

"I know that you will find your future in the past," the old man said, his voice croaky.

"Well, that must make great sense once you have had a drink or two. Hell, how about five or six shots? That should bring great clarity to a fool's meaning."

"Did you know that there is darkness on the summit of Benbulbin even when the sun shines upon it?"

Max did not know how to respond to what appeared to be a riddle. He simply stared and then answered, "Well, to be honest, I have not been on top of the mountain since I became an adult. Too sacred for me. I just know that it is a beautiful sight from Drumcliff even to those that do not understand the concept of beauty."

"I tell you what. I have a son that can take you to the summit. I live with him on her flank. We raise donkeys to sell to travelers. On nights of celebration, we take believers to the top."

"I am sure there must be a big demand for asses," said Max, trying to conceal his amusement. "By the way, what believers are you talking about? I have always heard that the mountain was sacred to the ancient ones. You know, the druids and other crazies."

"Don't make fun of what you do not know!" protested the old man in a loud voice. "The spirits only appear to those who have an 'O' in front of their last name."

"That leaves me out. Well, maybe not. Seems like my great-grandfather went by the name O'Shell. What a crock." He paused for a moment. "Forgive me, I have had a long day. I must appear very rude."

"Again here is my phone number," said O'Sullivan as he extended his trembling hand towards Max. "If you want to know what you must do, call me. It will be my son that answers."

"Sure, okay." Max finished his beer and began to leave the pub.

"Max," said his friend Thomas in a whisper, "I see you met O'Sullivan, the village prophet... or rather, the village idiot."

"Yeah, you really meet the most interesting people on the way to the john."

On his way back to the estate house, he could not help staring at Benbulbin. The setting sun was just striking the prow of the mountain. The fields of grass on its flanks bore the warm colors of an artist's palette as though the unseen was mixing them into various hues to be applied to a canvas of stone.

"That old fool O'Sullivan. What does he know of life? Only self-made hardships. I have to admit, however, that I am curious regarding the summit of the mountain," said Max to himself. "I might just give his son a call. Like hell I will."

THAT NIGHT MAX ONCE MORE HAD TROUBLE SLEEPING. He tried to remember his various extramarital affairs but his thoughts only ended fitfully. He arose and walked to the kitchen hoping to find some milk to soothe his stomach and induce a peaceful sleep. He opened the oversized refrigerator and lifted the large milk jar from its secure position. He looked at the label only to notice that it had expired the previous week. Furious, he slammed the refrigerator closed. Distraught, he listened to the sounds of the house and the murmur of the ocean that lay at its foundation. The sea was as restless as he.

Having once more shrouded himself in the refuge of his bed's covers, he listened to the waves striking the beach. Soon sleep captured him defenseless. He saw Benbulbin in all of its shades of green. Colors streaked past in high-speed animation. Then suddenly all was still. The top of the mountain began to burn. Figures began to dance about a stone in the shape of an inverted Celtic cross. The figure mounted upon the stone was he.

Max struggled to awaken. He quickly found himself sitting upright in bed. His body was burning hot; sweat ran down his brow and dampened his pajama top. He wanted to run to his mother like a child would, yet he knew she was not there. A deep aching sense of loss filled his body.

He got up and walked down the long hall, then knocked on Nancy's door. She was awake but did not answer him. He entered the quiet room and stared at her figure clothed in moonlight. He pulled back her covers and slipped into the bed. He did not touch her but lay on his side silently, listening to the sea and the wind that sought entrance to the chamber.

Then slowly he rolled over to her side pressing her body against his own. Then he climbed upon her motionless form and entered her. He climaxed quickly as though it were a part of a dream. A dreamless sleep soon followed.

Outside the window the dawn began to appear, at first only a hint of color added to the gray sky. Swiftly the sky turned to a pyrrole-red rouge. Then a bird began its song in the oak tree just outside the window. He arose, careful not to awaken Nancy. He did not want to explain why he had sought her comfort when his fear came only from a dream.

After a breakfast in which he ate alone, he dialed the number that O'Sullivan had given him in the pub. The phone rang several times indicating that there was no answering machine monitoring the line and then the receiver was lifted gently from its cradle.

"Hello, this is Samuel Shell calling. I now go by Max. Do I have the pleasure of speaking to a Mr. O'Sullivan?" Even though the phone had been lifted from its cradle, no one responded. "Hello, is anyone there?"

A strong youthful voice replied, "Who is calling me on such a day that foretells only storms?"

"Like I said earlier, this is Max Shell. Your father, Mr. O'Sullivan, told me that you transported people to the top of Benbulbin."

"I might do that occasionally. What are you looking for up there? Some history or maybe even a sorcerer? You know, after all that hoopla about mystical shit in the movies, you get all kinds of crazies wanting to see the top of the mountain, especially in the rain. Nothing there except some stone carvings."

"Well, that is what I am interested in." Max did not want to reveal to anyone that he was searching for answers related to the death of his teenage son. He realized that no one in the world that he knew could provide a true response, only opinions.

After the death of Aran, he had buried himself in his work. While not a spiritual man, he often thought about the possibility that the soul exist. In his youth, he was trained to be a good Catholic by his mother. Yet he had grown to be like the tigers in the circus, obedient but angry at her whip of words.

His grandmother often mentioned the spirits of the departed who roamed the earth. These were fascinating stories to him, but they remained only legends. *If only I can tell Aran that I love him... if only,* he thought.

"One of those archeology types?" The voice of O'Sullivan's son startled him.

"You might say that. Your father got me interested in the summit of the mountain. He said that I might find what I have been looking for up there among the crags."

"Really, my father tends to exaggerate things. He is the kind that still believes in fairies and the banshee."

"Are you kidding me? I heard a lot about the banshee when I was very young. To be honest, I have not thought of one in several years. If I remember correctly, she can appear in many forms."

"Yah, so can the Easter Bunny," Tim O'Sullivan replied.

"I know my Irish grandmother used to describe her as a pale woman with red hair," replied Max. "Seems like she always appears wearing a white dress. You know, the virginal whore look."

"I think that my old man saw her a couple of times on the mountain when he was young and drunk. He didn't ask you to pay a visit to her, did he?"

"Well, not exactly. He didn't describe her as a banshee, just as a person."

"I will take you up there on an ass provided it doesn't start raining. If you want my advice, just take some pictures. We will want to be down before any thunderstorms arrive. If we are not down by mid-afternoon, we will be acting as lightning rods. You never want to be caught on an Irish mountain in the dark. You will slide straight to hell if you slip."

"Okay, tell me how to get to your house."

THE ROAD TO O'FLANNAN'S WAKE was very winding with sharp switchbacks. When Max arrived at O'Sullivan's house, he sat for a moment in the car. Against the face of the mountain, large cumulous clouds had gathered. There was a fresh pasture odor in the air, part wet dung and grass.

O'Sullivan's yard had free-range chickens and behind his marred white stone house was a killing vat for hogs. Peering over the wire fence were several small burros chewing their cuds. A large sheep dog barked from the house. Soon a door opened and the dog ran to Max's car, immediately urinating on a tire while continuing to bark.

"See you made it to the house," said Tim O'Sullivan.

"Must be my lucky day. I don't see how you make it if it rains," remarked Max.

"Don't go nowhere if it rains. Nothing down the mountain anyway."

"Your point of view isn't shared by many," responded Max.

"I'm not like my father who loves a cold Guinness, raw oysters and a woman's buttocks to look at. No sir, just want to be here tending my sheep herds. I have what I want, and it is right here."

"Seems like I heard the same line from your father."

"You will have to pay for two donkeys. I am sure as shit not walking." Tim then vanished inside the barn and brought forth two gray-brown donkeys.

"Tim, where are the saddles?" asked Max.

"Don't have any. That is what these blankets are for," Tim replied as he hurled a thick woven blanket towards Max who caught it in midair.

"Your dad referred to the animals as burros."

"Sounds better than asses. Tourists like the Latino name."

SLOWLY THEY FOLLOWED THE SWITCHBACKS UP THE MOUNTAIN. The brilliant red of the dawn had turned into a sullen gray that threatened rain at every moment of their ascension. The animals walked at a slow but steady pace along the switchbacks on the face of Benbulbin.

After a laborious ride, Tim stopped and dismounted. "Well, Professor, now we climb the bastard. I sure hope you are not wearing street shoes."

"You mean we cannot ride all the way to the top?" Max responded.

"Hell no. You see that gully in front of you? It is called the Pinnacle Gully."

"Surely there is another way!"

"Yah, but not a spiritual way, and that is what you are after says my father."

Max followed Tim up the slippery gully, now moistened by mist, gripping pieces of slate-colored rocks as often as he could.

He would place the sole of his boot on a stone, rock back and forth for a moment to see if it would dislodge, and then place his weight on it. In this slow methodical method, he climbed far behind Tim on his way to the summit. Then, as if by magic, they arrived at the plateau. Before him was a treeless undulating environment crisscrossed by countless streams.

"There is nothing here," said Max, still breathing heavily.

"There is if you listen and open your ears. The fairies are here you know. Since you have climbed their mountain, they will pursue you. In a dream, you will learn the truth about your son."

Max looked at Tim. "How did you know about my son?"

"They visit me, too," he responded and then laughed shaking his head.

A FOG-LIKE CLOUD WAS NOW EMBRACING the limestone mountain, the child of ancient glaciers. With the cloud came a chilly wind followed by rain. Max stood looking at the desolate plateau of peat. In the distance, partially hidden by fog, a small procession of people appeared slowly walking, one following another.

"Tim! Look over there," Max said as he pointed towards the small procession.

"What? I don't see anything but fog and clouds born of an Atlantic storm."

"People, look at them!"

"What people? Just fog and cloud, nothing there, guvnor."

"No, wait… See? They are walking towards that group of large stones."

"You mean the monolith? Just a bunch of rocks."

Max began to walk swiftly towards the people. As he walked, he did not notice coming too close to one of the many streams that crossed the summit. Suddenly he fell into its icy waters.

Max moved his legs frantically in a kicking motion. He expected to touch the bottom since the small meandering streams, just moments before, seemed so shallow. He flailed his arms after breaking the surface. Max felt confident that his companion would see him and immediately come to his assistance. He waited, but the severe cold of the stream caused him to plummet into its depths. Suddenly before him was Aran. He could see him in the clear cold water. Seaweed was wrapped about his torso. Aran swam towards him very slowly, taking his hand and placing it upon a slippery limestone rock that protruded from the side of the stream. His son then smiled at him and floated backwards into the depth of the deep ice-green water.

A voice from above shouted, "Mr. Shell, what the hell are you doing? The water is only two feet deep and you are acting as if you are drowning. Come on, give me your hand and I will pull you out like I would a frightened child."

Max struggled along the slippery embankment, falling again into the shallow water. He could not believe that now he could sit upright in the flowing stream. He placed his hands on the rocky bottom as though attempting to penetrate the stone in an effort to prove that he was not hallucinating.

"Man, I have never seen anything like this is in all of my days of guiding people up this mountain. You act like you have just seen a banshee or something."

"Tim, this water was very deep just a moment ago. I swear to you!"

"Yah, deep enough to drown a rat in."

"No, I am serious," said Max in a voice that he himself did not recognize.

"Tell you what, Professor – you are hallucinating due to cold-water shock."

"I tell you I saw my son!" said Max as he attempted to force air from his lungs.

"Like hell you did, Professor. Come on. You have to lie down in the water to drown. There is no way that you could have seen anyone. I was looking at you the whole time. I would have pulled you out sooner, but you kept jerking and acting like you were swimming. Like I said before, I have never seen anything like it before in my life. We need to get you off the mountain and set you by my father's fire."

At that moment, rain began to fall heavily upon the two lone figures that struggled to walk together. The rain soon reduced the visibility.

"Before we descend the gully, we need to let it slacken off a little," said Tim with concern in his voice.

Both men sat on the overlook silently. Tim produced a pipe from his pocket and managed to light it despite the downpour. The wide brim of his hat provided shelter to the flame as he inhaled the aromatic tobacco smoke.

When the rain abated enough for them to walk safely, Tim guided Max down the gully by instinct. His hands found stones to grip and acted independently of his thought processes. It was as though his body was guiding him without any direction from his inner self. Like an animal, he moved slowly but deliberately.

IT WAS NOT LONG UNTIL THEY WERE SEATED by the peat fire that his father had lit. The elder O'Sullivan offered Max some warm clothing, then covered his shoulders with a deep red woolen blanket.

"Mr. O'Sullivan," said Max, "I saw Aran or at least I think so."

"Sometimes we see things that are not really there. I must admit, however, that there is something about Benbulbin that none of us can explain. Even Father O'Hare, who is the best historian in the area, can't come up with an answer for everything that takes place on that mountain. Only people searching for something should ever go up there. Majority of the people who climb it don't find what they are looking for. Mostly English and Americans who have no faith," Mr. O'Sullivan said, winking at his son who only smiled in acknowledgement.

"While you were changing, Tim told me that you nearly drowned in a small stream. Lord knows, there are a lot of them up there. Couldn't have been more than a meter deep. He told me that all you had to do was sit up. I guess that people can drown in a drizzle. You know a turkey can." With that comment, Tim and his father once more exchanged smiles.

Max looked directly at his host. "Mr. O'Sullivan, I saw something else while I was up there. A small procession of people in the distance just before I fell into the stream. Do you have any idea who they were?" Max said in an almost pleading voice.

"All kinds of people hike up there. Did Tim see them?"

Tim glanced away from the fire. "No, Father, there was nothing there but fog. I think that Mr. Shell mistook a rock for a group of people."

"There you have it," replied the older O'Sullivan. "It was all a trick of the mind. At least, that is what it is to my son. As for me, I believe that what you saw was real, just in a different dimension."

"What might that dimension be?" replied Max who renewed his shaking from the damp cold that still resided within him.

"Well, you saw into the spirit world. The world of the ancient ones, the druids or such as they are called. To say more would be to blaspheme the Church." The elder O'Sullivan stared at him and said no more about the subject.

Outside the rain was slackening yet the air remained very cold. Distant clouds continued to hide the summit of the mountain. Max dressed himself in his still damp clothes and pushed against the red wooden door. "I want to thank you both. I have encouragement now, something that I did not have before. Perhaps I was foolish to go after that which I have found even if the meaning remains unclear. I now know that it is possible to seek and to find."

"Professor, be careful," the older O'Sullivan said surprisingly loud. "You are dealing with things that you do not understand. I suggest that you talk to Father O'Hare if you want to know more about yourself, the mountain and what you seek. He is a wise man even if he seldom smiles."

MAX RETURNED TO HOLBROOK where once more the clouds had grown darker and the drizzle had turned into a steady heavy rain. He ran out of the car without bothering to open his umbrella. Fortunately, the door was not locked. He entered the great hallway. At the far end of the second flight of stairs, a large stained-glass window bore mythical images of ancient Ireland, the famous bull portrayed in the Táin Bó Cúailnge. There upon the summit depicted in the painting was a procession, similar to that he had seen.

"I must seek out Father O'Hare to see what insight he can provide."

THE DRIVE TO THE CHURCH WAS A PLEASANT ONE. The hedgerows

with their abundant fruits, herbs and flowers charmed him. He lowered the windows of his Mercedes to allow the fresh scents of the countryside to enter. Max then lowered the roof since the sun promised no showers. The quiet sound of the engine allowed him to enjoy the larks that flew about the hedgerows in pursuit of their love.

The small stone church was located near the flank of the mountain near a stream that flowed from the summit. There were many stone markers about the church. To Max it appeared that there had been little attention to the placement of graves. Away from the church, were small stones that marked the graves of unbaptized infants.

The pavement stopped and flat stones provided the remainder of the drive to the church. He parked his car and looked into the darkened sanctuary where small thin openings provided the illumination for the church. In the distance was a beautiful altar adorned with only a few candles. Outside the main building, were the ruins of what appeared to be an ancient monastery now roofless, typical of so many sites in Ireland.

Max entered the Church where he was greeted with the odors of wet stone, peat and stagnant rainwater. Suddenly Father O'Hare appeared next to him like an apparition.

"Father, Mr. O'Sullivan said that you were the local expert on Benbulbin. Oh, excuse me, my name is Max Shell."

"Are you kin to Mary O'Flaherty who lived at Cleggan?"

"Yes, she was my grandmother. How did you make the association?"

"You look a great deal like her. I remember her in my youth. A beautiful woman with angular features and very black hair. A real charmer in her day. Of course, I am a priest and could not express that to her then. I only wish that I could have. It might have stopped her from marrying your grandfather. I am sorry. Forgive an old man who speaks before he thinks."

"Father, in the house that I purchased on the beach – Holbrook, that is – there is a stained-glass window that bears the image of Benbulbin. On the summit depicted in the glass, there appears to be a procession. Can you tell me more about it?"

"Well, you are the first man that has ever asked me about it. Well, that be damned Cromwell had ordered the execution of loyal Irishman. He wanted them hung on the summit so that all could either see their bodies or would hear about them. What he didn't know was that he was making them a legend. Yes, the cursed one made them immortal. What you see depicted is the procession of condemned men bearing their own crosses. Yes, just like in the Bible."

"Father, I saw a procession of men carrying heavy objects when I was on the summit of the mountain. Mr. O'Sullivan's son, who was my guide, did not see them."

"He was not supposed to, only a descendent of one of those men are so gifted. You saw not them but their guardian angels."

"Thank you, Father." Max could not help but feel that the priest had grown senile.

"My son, be careful. Let the past bury the past. You are still young. You have seen a miracle. Let that be enough."

UPON RETURNING TO THE ESTATE, MAX CHECKED his e-mail. He had earlier requested a DNA study on his father's side. He had long heard stories by his mother that one of his distant relatives was black. He had long assumed that the term "Black Irish" referred only to the color of the hair.

The possibility that he had a historical connection to Africa intrigued him ever since he heard the tale of his biological history.

When he inquired more, his grandmother only said that it was a family story, nothing more. A mere product of too many fireside chats.

After hearing of a friend's DNA test, he decided to be tested, too. A simple swab on the inside of his cheek would settle the issue once and for all. In his mailbox, he found a notification that the results of the DNA test were available.

At first he was excited but then he realized that it was more difficult to interpret the results than he had imagined. As he began to read, there were references to Africa, but they were related to the common conclusion that all mankind had originated there. His relationship to Africa remained as it had before, a blank canvas, fertile ground only for the imagination.

The majority of his family tree showed that he was descended from Irish, English and Scotch. Then after reading further down the list, it stated that there was a more recent DNA connection to Africa. While not a larger percentage of DNA showed any African descent, it was enough to explain why his eyes and skin were darker than most of his friends. His skin was of an olive complexion and his eyes a very deep brown.

"It must have been the involvement of my distant relative in the slave trade at the time. Just like the English, making a profit from the suffering of other people."

That night, he lay awake wondering about the person who married a woman of Africa. As he tossed, he thought about the woman. Was she beautiful or plain? What region of Africa did she come from and how did she meet the person that he was descended from? Was it love or a forced relationship? Answers to these questions were not available from the DNA report. The part of the story that interested him most was missing.

CHAPTER NINE
Analysis of an Affair

An Affair Now Told

You were there, a painting of desire.
Passion seen in the blue of the flame.

Weakness revealed by strength alone.
The mask of kindness seen without.
Too soon to confront that which dwells within.

A wise man a fool revealed.
Where strength is shown, a jester dwells.

MAX WAS INVITED TO ADDRESS A CONFERENCE in Washington D.C. The invitation necessitated his leaving Ireland a week earlier than anticipated. Nancy and Margaret decided to stay the last week of their scheduled trip in Dublin where they could do more shopping on Grafton Street.

The conference that Max was to attend dealt with the development of future leaders in the field of international affairs. He would not have accepted such an invitation if it had not been for one of his junior executives, Ms. Karen Maddox.

Karen was a graduate of Harvard's business school and had published in *Harvard Review*. When she applied for the job, she was straightforward in her desire for a leadership position. Max had too often found a lack of leadership traits in his recent interviewees for senior management positions. It seemed that most applicants had only a nine-to-five mentality. They sought lengthy vacations and early retirement. They wanted to know what the company could do for them. In other words, none of that J. F. K. crap of what can you do for your country.

She was very different. She had sat there with her light-gray business suit, short skirt and fashionable shoes. Karen appeared to be a dyed blond or at least he thought so. He envied her youthful self-confidence – a trait that he had earlier possessed in his own business career. But most of all, she maintained direct eye contact. Something that he admired in any associate. It told him that this person would be forthright and honest. These were traits that he expected in any person whether a professional, friend or lover.

THE CONFERENCE WAS TO BE HELD AT THE WEIDMARK HOTEL. A virtual landmark to conference attendees. It was an older hotel situated near a park that fronted on the Potomac River. The Lincoln

Memorial and other buildings dedicated to the success of capitalism could be seen across the river at night.

Max debarked from his taxi that had just taken him from Dulles International. He unloaded his large, somewhat antiquated suitcases with their large handles and squeaky wheels. Outside, a small remnant of the moon remained, producing only a symbol of moonlight.

Standing at the front desk was Karen. Her blond hair was in a loose ponytail that hung down to her waist and pointed towards her hips. Her tight skirt was the first thing that he noticed.

She could sense that someone was staring at her, an uncomfortable stare that at first irritated her. Karen turned swiftly around. "Mr. Shell," she said somewhat surprised, "I am glad that your journey was a safe one. I must admit that the traffic from the airport was heavier than I had expected." She paused as the clerk handed her information about the hotel. "I must have arrived just before you did."

He could smell the rich odor of Shalimar perfume that floated in the air around her. Max felt somewhat awkward as he waited for her to be assigned a room. "Karen, I hope that you will join me for a drink once you are comfortable in your room."

Karen paused and then looked at him. "I will be happy to join you. Where and when should we meet?

"I know a small Lebanese restaurant not too far from here. They serve very good food and excellent drinks. Would seven-thirty be all right with you? I will be waiting here in the lobby."

"Yes, that will be fine. That will give me time to answer several e-mails. As you so well know, we can never be free of the world around us," Karen said with a smile.

EARLY IN HIS CAREER, HE HAD STAYED at the Weidmark and found it much to his liking. It was a substantial building filled with dark wood interiors and tall ceilings. He enjoyed the light breeze provided by the ornamental ceiling fans. Quiet ambient music could be heard throughout the foyer and halls. In the evenings, a piano played light classical in the main foyer. The Weidmark did not have the awkward appearance so common in new hotels, like florescent lights disguised in plastic plants.

The staff walked in front of him as he entered the elevator, their faces conveying their indifference to their job. Upon placing the valises on the luggage rack in the room, Max generously tipped them. He remembered failing to tip the cabin steward on the ship on his own honeymoon to Paradise Island when the island was no more than a mere sandbar. His wife's black negligee had gone missing from their stateroom when they returned from breakfast. He knew that it had been deliberately taken, but why? When he complained to the bursar, it was quickly determined that if he provided the bursar with a tip, the negligee would be returned.

Later, on the same trip, he had failed to tip the driver of the hotel shuttle. From then on, they were forced to walk over the bridge into Nassau. He remembered how simple and carefree their lives had been in that former British Crown colony so many years ago. Before the wealth, the affairs, the emptiness that now filled his soul. How he wished he could return to that summer so long ago when they were graduate students filled with all the optimism of change so prevalent in the 1970s. Anything and everything was possible.

Prior to meeting Nancy, Lt. Max Shell had returned from Vietnam. He knew that if he were to fulfill his own ambition regarding success, he would need to serve in the military, preferably in combat. Despite his youth, he had a broad understanding of life. Before meeting Nancy, he had been in love with a girl who worked in the Wan Chai district of Hong Kong. She had been a hostess at the Bar Plaza. A forbidden romance to those in his position of rank and authority.

He had promised to return for her, but in that time period promises were made to be broken. Everything was deemed irrelevant, even love itself. What was important to his generation was change.

As he sat in the room at the Weidmark, his past inexplicably bothered him. He thought about his love for Kam-Mui. She had been sold to the Bar Plaza by her family. She was not a common prostitute but a young woman in a situation that she could not control. A victim in a victimizing society. Perhaps it was not love but pity that made him feel compassion for her. He knew better for it was love that drew him to her. It was love that now prevented him from forgetting her.

After reading the *Wall Street Journal*, he looked at himself in the mirror. At times, he felt that he was looking at a stranger, an apparition separate and apart from who he truly was.

WHEN HE ARRIVED EARLY IN THE LOBBY, Karen was already waiting for him. He admired that in a person inferior to him in position.

"Karen are you ready to dine?" he asked, looking down at her.

She looked up at him and smiled.

They walked from the Weidmark to the Lebanese restaurant as though they were strangers, not touching. He opened the door for her and held two fingers up towards the host.

"Sir, do you have reservations?" asked the greeter.

"No, but these do," he said, presenting the host with two hundred dollar bills.

"Yes sir, I have your table available now. Please follow me."

The other guests who were waiting in line looked at Max and

marveled with a degree of bitterness at the prompt service that he had received.

"Karen, what would you like to order?" he said quietly.

"What do you recommend?" she asked, staring at the menu and turning over several pages.

"If I remember correctly, the mouzat is very good."

"I always like to know what I am ordering," she said in a very professional voice.

"I am sorry. It is braised lamb shank over tomato sauce. It is traditionally served with rice."

"I will have the same," she said.

"What beverage would you and the lady prefer?" asked the newly arrived sommelier.

Max hesitated and appeared to be thinking more for effect than lack of knowledge. He always gave much thought to any action that he was taking regardless of how trivial the matter was.

"A bottle of Massaya Gold Reserve red," replied Max.

"An excellent choice, sir."

She admired how smoothly he made decisions. He gave the appearance of acting from instinct rather than memorized facts. Even trivia was treated with great respect.

The waiter quickly returned with the gold-labeled bottle and proceeded to present the cork to Max who sniffed it briefly. "Excellent, it will do fine."

The waiter then proceeded to pour the wine into two tall crystal glasses that reflected the lights of the restaurant.

"I have enjoyed the foods, drinks and service of Maya's for many years. Even before I founded my land development company and other business interests, they treated me with an unearned respect so foreign in Washington D.C. It is nice to see a restaurant where servers take pride in their occupation. Now, Karen, please tell me more about yourself. I already know all the résumé material."

"Unfortunate for me and fortunate for you, I am divorced."

"I could only assume that. FERPA prevents asking of such personal questions."

"Would it have made any difference if I was still married?"

"Now you are asking me a very personal question. One that when answered, will reveal a great deal about myself. The answer to your question is no."

"Do all men have such a dark side to their personality?" she asked.

"How do I answer such a sweeping question? A holy man would surely say 'Yes, it makes a difference.'"

"Do you believe in holy men?" she asked as though seeking a truthful answer.

"Only one such man lived, and he was God," Max said.

"Oh, you mean Chairman of the Shell Corporation," she said, smiling.

"Then you believe that the dark side of man is universal," said Max as though seeking to rebut her earlier answer." She did not reply to his question. "What then ended your marriage? You do not need to answer if it makes you feel uncomfortable."

"Max, I really don't know. I think that in many ways we were compatible. We both loved to travel, entertain and sail. We had a very nice sailboat that we kept moored in Tampa, Florida. Nothing pretentious, just a nice boat to enjoy in the evenings when we visited relatives that had retired in nearby Sarasota. At one time, we even thought that we too would like to live there, but that was only a dream.

"We even wanted to have children but that never happened. Our careers kept getting in the way. We were both equally ambitious. Ambition can be a dangerous thing to a relationship," Karen said. "I think that if we could have had children, we would have stayed together."

She continued, "You must be waiting for me to tell you all the ways that my husband and I were different. Perhaps we were too much alike to stay in love. Too familiar with each others' habits. When I looked at him, I saw myself. Now tell me about you and your wife. Not everything is perfect or you would not have flirted with me."

"Flirted? Without being offensive to you, why must everything – every relationship – be about sex? Men are more than animals."

"Come on, Max. Be truthful. All you really want from me is to get me in bed with you tonight."

"Well, I do hope that we will make love. But more than that, I hope that we can talk," he said more seriously than he intended. Max knew that in any fledgling relationship, neither male nor female should act too seriously. How could he portray the role of a king when playing the part of a jester?

They sat in a small alcove of the restaurant looking deeply within one another's eyes. "Karen, not that I am counting, but how many glasses of wine have I bought you tonight?"

"Enough for a promotion, I hope," she said with a smile while hinting with her eyes that he needed to refill her glass.

"If I promoted you again, you would have my job," Max said, laughing. "Let us return to our previous conversation when we were honest yet cautious. Why don't you spend the night with me?"

"That is a possibility," she replied with a coquettish smile.

Max was stunned by her boldness. Then he felt irritated that she would be so forthright with her willingness to have an affair. He possessed a strange mixture of both desire and repulsion. It should not have been this easy for him. In life, everything came with only the asking.

"Tell me why you are unfaithful or at least hope to be," she said seriously.

"Please do not misinterpret me, an invitation to a bed is not a marriage proposal. I have loved my wife for the majority of my life. To me, sex is separate and apart from an enduring relationship. Sex is transitory at best. Love, when felt with the emotions of an artist, can be immortal."

"Come on, Max, you are just trying to justify your infidelity. Besides, what makes you think I would be any better in bed than Nancy? You were in the Navy and so was my ex-husband. I think that he, like you, was a tin can sailor. Well, to sum it up, you both have a girl-in-every-port mentality. A woman wants more than a man. A woman wants to feel pretty, listened to and loved all at the same time. A touch is important only if it conveys a sincere emotion of the heart. Words are more important to us. If men would only stop and speak to us before making love, then we would give love like they have never known before."

"You make me appear so shallow. Do you think that I do not want to love and to be loved? If sex leads to love, then so be it."

Karen looked at Max. "There is a tour of the precious gems museum tonight. I apologize, but I had already bought a ticket before my journey to Washington. Would you like to accompany me?"

At first Max hesitated as he studied the dark red wine within the crystal glass. "Yes, that will be fine. I have nothing else planned for the evening."

"Then good, the tour leaves at seven-thirty from the front of the Weidmark."

Though the food was too heavy for lunch, they both enjoyed the drinks and the conversation that followed. Max noticed that the more Karen drank, the more relaxed she became. Her cheeks turned warmer in the subdued light of the restaurant. He loved to look into her wide blue eyes as though they were a portal to her thoughts. A place where he could enter safely within.

He walked her back to the lobby of the hotel. They shook hands as they parted company.

THE TOUR OF THE SMITHSONIAN GEM and Mineral Collection housed at the Smithsonian's National Museum of Natural History was as he had expected. Indifferent historical stones on display before crowds that could not purchase them. Max, however was taken aback by her knowledge of the brilliant gems, especially the history of the owners.

He had always considered the lives of artists to be more fascinating than their works. There was one exception: Van Gogh's "Starry Night" captivated him. The emotion behind the colors and strokes fascinated him. There was something in the harshness of the application of the oils that he identified with. Perhaps he saw within himself the conflicts of the artist. He both loved and hated the painter. His talent was not something that could be bought. The greater the conflict, the closer to perfection he became. Van Gogh in his poverty had created something of enduring beauty. Out of the struggle had come the divine revelation of a feeling.

Returning on the shuttle to the hotel, Max placed his palm on her wool-covered leg. The material felt soft to him as the warmth of her flesh was conveyed through her skirt. She placed her hand over his as both of them looked at the lights above the Potomac.

"May I come to your room?" questioned Max.

"Yes, but first I want to freshen up," she said, gently letting go of his grasp.

AFTER TWO HOURS, HE CALLED HER ROOM. "What is your

number?" he asked.

Amused, she replied, "Room 232."

As he walked down the long lobby that was filled with mirrors and potted plants, he listen to Debussy's " Rêverie," a song that haunted him. The walls echoed his stride on the oak flooring of the hotel's corridors.

He knocked gently on the door.

"Come in, Max." She was wearing a bathrobe of white terrycloth. Her hair hung freely about her shoulders. The scent within the room was his beloved Shalimar. Just as he closed the door, there was another knock.

"Please excuse me, but I have a long-stem rose to deliver," said the member of the staff.

Max smiled at Karen. "I hope that you will accept this rose from me. I thought it would look good on your dresser and later on your bed."

"That is very romantic of you, Max. Few men arrive with a single flower."

He walked towards her and gently took her hand. "A rose not given simply dies and is forgotten. I did not want this evening to be forgotten."

He led her to the bed. He undid her bathrobe, allowing it to fall down her bare shoulders. He touched her breasts as he kissed her, first gently, and then with more passion.

They lay down on the bed facing one another. She could feel his passion against her. At first she felt reluctant, then she sought him. It was a passion that she was not used to with other men. As he raised himself to be on top of her, she pushed him down and mounted him with wild ferocity. The world, with its conflicts and indifference, ceased as their bodies pressed together, not with love but with the passion of two beasts.

CHAPTER TEN

A House in Connecticut

MAX LOOKED AT NANCY. "Why did we purchase this big house, full of antiques and yet empty of love? Oh, I now remember, you said that you wanted a fairy tale castle to live in yet close enough by car, train or air to both New York and Boston. You know, we now have a fairy tale house, but our lives together are far from being a fairy tale."

Their estate consisted of two hundred acres surrounded by forests and fences made of stone. Within the formal gardens were statues carved from Italian marble. Beyond the gardens were acres of mowed grass maintained as a private golf course and, further away, a paved landing strip to accommodate a private jet.

Homes of this type were seldom lived in for more than a few weeks a year. They were places to entertain the rich and famous, maintained by a small staff who, when needed, waited upon every need of the latest arrivals. Business colleagues, politicians and rock stars frequented the great homes of the area.

A paved driveway surrounded by large oaks led the guests to the great house. It was Edwardian in style with gray limestone walls, slate roofing and multiple flues. The mansion gave the impression that it had just been delivered by FedEx from England's Lake District.

Max employed a beautiful, young, ambitious estate manager, Mary Kathleen O'Connor. She was Irish in bloodline and mannerisms. He loved her confidence and, most of all, her blue eyes and deep red hair that hung carelessly about her shoulders.

While eluding sexuality, she was brilliant. A graduate of Brown with an MBA from MIT, she had presented him with a sterling resume and a radiant smile. Her short skirt and beautifully tanned legs made him say yes to her more than he intended to. Her judgment, however, regarding the management of the estate was impeccable. Mary could arrange parties and accommodate guests on a moment's notice. Her salary was far above any of the other property managers in the area and, therefore, he was able to keep her employed. Another reason that she had not left the area for one of the nearby metropolises was that her husband was from Salisbury. He was a plain person filled with good intent, yet nothing significant had come from his efforts.

"My god," said Max to Mary, "all he can do is deliver petroleum in a truck not yet paid for and coach a peewee league baseball team! I can't believe that you stay with him."

Mary fixed her eyes upon his. "Max, are you making me a better offer?"

Even though he managed a large business empire in which he did not hesitate to dismiss an employee, he was weak before a beautiful woman.

"No, no, Mary, I did not mean any offense. I was just thinking out loud. I think you deserve more in life than what he is able to give you."

"Max, that is nice of you to say. Maybe someday you will have the courage to really speak what is on your mind. Like you, I am always ready to upgrade. Until then, Fredie will do just fine. A lap dog is always needed on a winter's night."

Mary was also the antagonist between Nancy and Max. Nancy was well aware of Max's attraction to her. She knew that Mary could have anything she wanted. She knew within her heart that Max would never love her but only use her as one would an object where desire and possession was the same thing. That thought was the only comfort that Nancy had remaining to her for she could not compete physically with Mary's youth or stamina. She knew that Max was attracted to ambitious women yet he was afraid of them at the same time. He fully realized their willingness to bring a lawsuit against him since many of them were Ivy League law school graduates. His only defense against sexual harassment lawsuits was his team of lawyers, and yet he did not fully trust them either. Like in his relationship to his priest, he wanted to believe in them but could not.

Stone Creek Lodge was more than an estate – it was perfection to those who did not know the lives of its inhabitants. The nineteenth-century iron and stone entryway was adorned with alabaster deer heads with brass antlers and constantly monitored by two security cameras. Those who drove past assumed that the inhabitants of such pastoral seclusion had to be fulfilled and happy. Not to be in such a state of grace would be a sin.

Even though they felt a great void between each other, Max and Nancy enjoyed the warmth of the fireplace. The comfort of sitting in their estate house looking at the fire and at each other, wondering if this was truly it – all that remained of a twenty-five-year marriage.

Max looked at Nancy. "I feel like I am suffocating in this house. The weather is cloudy and the fields are wet. It is May and it feels like October. Damn it, surely there is some place better than this!"

"Do you want to go to the city and eat at Frederick's?" asked Nancy.

"What on earth for? The food here is excellent. Besides I am gaining too much weight. Bad for the heart. What if I get diabetes? Believe it or not, I am tired of eating. Yes, tired of food in general. The menu is always the same regardless of how much French or Italian is used in the description. Why can't I just order red wine instead of choosing among fifteen varieties that all taste the same? Then some shit ass wants me to smell the cork. What on earth for? I love it when they swish it in a glass and ask for your approval to pour. I say, treat the damn thing just like you would a Coke regardless of where it is bottled."

Max continued as he increasingly became more upset, "Tipping, now that is a subject unto itself. Why don't the restaurants pay their employees enough to live on? I don't tip a person that sells me underwear or hardware. Why must I pay a waitress just because she does her duty? If you ask me, the owners of restaurants are the cheapest entrepreneurs of all."

"Max, I am sorry. I just wanted to make a suggestion. I know how bored you get just sitting here. Why don't you call Paul over to play a round of golf?"

"Paul, now that is a story of greed. The only reason he ventures over here is to try to steal the forty acres that adjoins his estate. When you are wealthy, you can't have a friend."

"Max, you used to enjoy people. What changed you?"

"Nancy, you know damn well what changed us both," he shouted.

"I did not cause Aran's death," Nancy said in a voice filled with pain. "It was your fault that he died. You could never admit that he was autistic. We could have intervened early in his life but you ignored my pleading. His lack of perfection in your eyes drove him to suicide. If only you had reached out to him before it was too late."

"Damn you, I didn't do anything wrong! All he needed was someone to be tougher on him than I was. It was you that wouldn't let him play sports. No way, you said, no football, no basketball, no swimming – nothing that, as you put it, 'endangered' him. What he was growing up into was a candy-ass coward."

Nancy shook her head in disbelief. "You are the one that refused to acknowledge the clear signs of his exceptionality."

"'Exceptionality? What word game are you playing? And what were those exceptionalities, I might ask," Max replied strongly.

"Why are you asking me these questions now? Why didn't you ask me earlier when we still had an opportunity to make a difference in his life? You always did leave the hard decisions to me," she responded angrily.

"There were no clear signs! I know that I am repeating myself, but your stubbornness requires it," he shouted.

"Don't you remember when Molly visited with us? She told us both that Aran was a different child. She had worked with autistic children and adults in a private school in Boston. She pleaded with us to get help."

"You and your damn sister. There was nothing wrong with Aran. Anyone could see that."

"You call stimming normal? That incessant rocking back and forth? His failure to make eye contact? His holding his ears when other children cried in delight at a game? Those are classic symptoms, but your pride refused to acknowledge them. Your solution being 'time will take care of it.'"

"How do you know that Aran killed himself? Lots of teenagers drown," he said in a weaker voice.

"I agree, but not our Aran. He was afraid of water. There is no way that he would have gone near it except when he had no alternatives left. Your constant attention to detail, finding fault in everything that he attempted to accomplish." Nancy continued after drying her eyes, "In a way, I think he wanted to show you that he was not afraid of water or anything else."

"You call failing classes an accomplishment?" questioned Max. "A man cannot survive if he is not an achiever. You can't hide behind definitions that are found in a textbook. I don't give a damn about what some so-called expert says, my son could have achieved much, a great deal in fact."

Nancy looked at him. "I think that the last straw was when you told him that he was nothing but a goddamn failure and you were going to send him to a military academy." She continued after pausing, "You know that he was at the high-end of autism. In fact, many children like him are gifted. You simply refused to see his gifts. He was artistic, something you cannot appreciate or understand."

"You mean he could have existed in the corporate world on poetry or sour notes on a piano? Come on, be serious."

Nancy replied, "Mr. Fresher said that he had a gift for playing the piano."

"All that I ever heard was his banging on the goddamn thing. How could I be in a room drowning in my work and have that noise going on? I thought autistic children hated noise."

"What do you know about music? I hope that someday when our lives have ceased and we are but spirits that you can ask him to forgive you. I pray that someday I might also be able to forgive you as well." She noted that his eyes were tearing as he looked away towards the immaculate fields of the estate. Before him was manmade perfection yet without love. Since Aran had died, there were only arguments or silence between them.

Max knew that he could not win an argument with Nancy regarding the fate of their son. Instead he returned to the previous topic. "The sons of bitches like Paul. Those are the ones that I can't stomach. The greed of others. Can't trust anyone when you have money. Besides, I noticed how he looked you over when we played tennis with him and his plastic wife, Denise. She has had almost as many facelifts as you have. I don't know what he wants more – my forty acres or your ass."

Nancy looked at him sternly. "At least he looks at me. Something you no longer do. I remember when you could not get enough of me." She paused. Avoiding eye contact so he would not take it as a challenge, a prelude to verbal combat, she continued, "Max, I didn't mean to offend you. My question about us going to the city was only an inquiry and not a statement about life."

Nancy had earlier suggested that they spend a week on Saint George Island before going to their condominium in Maui, Hawaii. A condominium built to the perfection of architectural standards, teak overstuffed furniture and polished bamboo floors. An original painting by Paul Gauguin was suspended on the paneling in his study. Sweeping glass walls with the ever-present salt that resided upon them faced the surf. Beyond the breaking waves, the cobalt blue of deep water could be seen.

"Perhaps a trip to Saint George would change everything, perhaps," she whispered to herself.

CHAPTER ELEVEN
St. George Island

HEAVY SUITCASES WERE SOON FILLED with unnecessary items. Their bags were packed and loaded into the SUV by their staff member, Alfred. Alfred was a young man just waiting to return to Boston College in the fall. His attending Boston College was one reason that Max had hired him.

"Nancy, have you remembered everything?" shouted Max.

"You know, it is your responsibility to pack your own things," she said sharply without looking at him.

HIGHWAY 95 THAT FOLLOWED THE COAST down to Florida was devoid of interest unless a detour was made to one of the barrier islands moored just off the eastern coasts of the Carolinas and Georgia.

"Max, it has been years since we walked on the beach in North Carolina. Cape Hatteras is not too far from the interstate. Let's be wild like we used to be and do something different."

"Nancy, that is a good suggestion," he replied unexpectedly. "I love Hatteras. Just think of all the excellent ships that lie at her bottom. No one planned on dying there, always the result of someone's mistake. Perhaps a captain wanting to make a deadline, a miscalculation regarding the weather. In some cases, perhaps all, a man's need to make port in order to be with his wife or lover. That must be it; a man's judgment is always clouded by a woman. It is our weakness."

"Max, you are really great at blaming others. It is as though you think that every bad decision you made was forced on you by either me or another female. Is there ever a time when you admit that you are a grown man and responsible for what happens to both you and me? You are the epitome of the dark side of man."

She could not believe he agreed to go to Hatteras with her. Perhaps she would not have suggested it had she known that he would be so agreeable to the idea. He was much more prone to reject her ideas than to support them.

THE SKY WAS A CLEAR SKY-BLUE IN COLOR. It was as though the ocean had covered them from above. She thought how the small white clouds looked like the frothing heads of waves that fall upon the shorelines of the world.

Before long they arrived at the Cape Hatteras National Park. Sea oats grew wild upon the dunes. In that it was a weekday, there were only a few day tourists to be seen. The campgrounds were sparsely occupied. They felt like they did when they were first in love. Max lowered the windows of the SUV, allowing the scent of the beach to enter the vehicle and their lungs.

Nancy smiled at him. "Max, thank you for taking me to this beach. The sun felt so warm and friendly when we were young and desired nothing more than each other's company. We worried about so little. Everything was ahead of us and I was very happy. There is no way to recapture those precious moments of youth. I cannot yet grasp how quickly the years have passed by. I think that I will awake and find myself being held by you on the beach. Under your wing like a small chick protected by its mother."

Max for one brief moment looked tenderly at her. "Yes, those were wonderful times. I would be willing to give up all that we have to recapture those fleeting moments here on this beach." He then placed his hand on her leg and said no more as they both stared at the sea and remembered what had been.

They had planned on enjoying the opportunity to visit with friends first in Sarasota and then in Tampa. From there, they would drive to Saint George Island.

"Max, I know that you planned on visiting with your friends on our trip. Why don't we go ahead to Saint George and let it be just the two of us?"

"Nancy, I get so few opportunities to visit with my former classmates and play golf," he said, looking towards the breakers.

At that moment, Nancy touched him as she had when they first met. "I think I can persuade you to continue to Saint George."

Max looked at her knowing that her embrace could change everything. He felt diminutive in his weakness. He did not take her on the beach in North Carolina for he wanted it to be perfect on Saint George.

WHEN HE WAS YOUNG, ST. GEORGE WAS A PLACE filled with fun in the carefree interlude of youth. A time of beach ball and strolls along the shell-strewn beach. As a couple, they would arise early before other beachcombers could find the most beautiful shells. For miles they would walk in the twilight before the rising sun glistened on the impatient waves of the Gulf of Mexico. Their laughter was heard like the cry of gulls that swept low over the breaking waves.

At night they would stand on the porch that faced the sea, holding each other and taking sips of the white wine that rested on the salty wood of the table. Later the stars would appear like jewels against a black cloth of the finest of weave. Then they would kiss boldly in the moonlight. Soon Nancy would lead him to their bed where their love was passionate and unrestricted.

He thought about those nights as they drove south to Apalachicola, the gateway to Saint George. Apalach, as he called it, was a small fishing community that had dried their nets in pursuit of tourists who arrived in ever greater numbers. When Max and Nancy had first traveled there, many of the buildings were abandoned or closed.

Max had discovered the area by looking at a map. Its many rivers and small islands impressed him with the potential for beachcombing and fishing. When he first saw it, he knew that it was the perfect spot to be. A place where two lovers could be alone. When they were silent, the waves became their voices.

St. George Island was very different from the mountains and exotic fragrances of Hawaii. A barrier island just off the coast of Florida and seaward of the unchanging fishing village of Apalachicola, Florida. An island whose exact dimensions depended too much upon the hurricane season that stretched from June until late October when giant erratic storms form off the coast of equatorial Africa threatened. In the real estate offices, plots were still recorded on the survey maps even though the sea had reclaimed them.

It is but a small island formed by the moving sands of the gulf, a barrier island that protects the coastal town of Apalachicola. On the island, there is no solid foundation on which to build the tall indifferent condominiums. The island with its small groves of coastal oak, pines and cedar sits bleached in the subtropical sun. Seabirds wade in small lagoons and await the castoff from the oyster boats and other small vessels that travel the Intercoastal Waterway.

The surf of the island is filled with the castoffs of the sea, not ideal for tourists seeking an idyllic location. The beach water is murky. When wading in the surf, myriad waves of seashells touch the feet and legs. Yet only hundreds of yards from the beach, the sea is clear and sparkles in its purity.

The shore with the falling tide in the early morning hours wears a coat of myriad seashells. Mollusks of all types are cast upon its beach and ground into sand or cast back into the sea to roll about in the returning waves. Nothing can endure the sea. Whatever it touches, it recreates in its own image.

THEY DROVE PAST THE LONG COLONNADE OF PINES that line the parkway just before they entered Apalachicola.

"Nancy, am I to be impressed by what I see?" remarked Max as he stared at the wooden-frame buildings of the small fishing port. "I hope to God the oysters are as good as the website said. At least I can enjoy eating and drinking. I suppose they have a local beer here just like all the other small coastal towns. I bet that it is their claim to fame. How anyone can drink the local stuff is beyond me. I remember one town calling their local brew 'Posthole Beer'. Can you image naming a beer that?"

Nancy did not reply but noticed the quaint boutique shops that lined the main street. When they had ventured there years before, most of the stores were closed. She remembered Max saying, "The only thing that sells around here are CLOSED signs."

Soon their car passed the Victorian-era Apalachicola Inn with its wide wraparound porch. Seated in rockers were middle-aged guests accompanied by their adult children and grandchildren. Nancy's eyes lingered on the smiles of the people as they talked to one another. A small toddler ran haphazardly down the wooden porch while his mother patiently pursued him, only to kiss him upon capture. She wanted to tell Max how happy the people were as they visited with one another, but she knew he would not understand. Empathy was only a word to him.

"Nancy, why we should go to such a desolate and very plain sea cottage when we have just recently purchased a very exclusive Hawaiian condominium at an exorbitant price is a question that I cannot answer."

Nancy knew that the condominium represented a gathering place for all their unfulfilled friends, a congregation of the lonely. Many traveled to visit them only to have a place to stay.

Nancy had a friend that retired near Disneyland. She complained that when she moved, her friends no longer wanted to visit her. The wealthy attracted others because of their ability to provide entertainment. Once their wealth vanished, they were as isolated as Irish cousins.

"We were happy on this island many years ago. You have probably forgotten all the times that we laughed. I even remember our smiles. We have fallen away from each other and need a place familiar to both of us. A sea cottage where we can talk and plan the rest of our lives together or apart. A cottage that stands alone from the others and faces the ocean. A place of driftwood and salt-scented air. A beach of shells and strangers. Sea Dreams was such a place, or at least it used to be."

"Nancy, do you think that such a place really exists? Such a place only resides within your thoughts."

As their car passed the Intercoastal Waterway, Nancy looked

down at the fishermen with their oyster tongs. She could see that the many wooden boats with crews of family members of all ages working together in the heat of the day. Their deeply tanned skin reflecting the traditions of their fathers. The water sparkled in the sun while warm weather clouds sailed above the small vessels.

THE CAR CROSSED THE BRIDGE that connected Saint George Island to the mainland. They thought once more about the beach cottage that they had shared in their youth. They knew that time changed everything but not the sea. Would it remain as it had always been in their dreams? The ocean conveyed within each person a different identity. No two people can see it the same way or experience a similar emotion when embraced by its wind and wave.

How glorious, she thought, *to be able to work together to accomplish something as simple as living. There is no jealousy among those who work together for a common good. How different from the world that I know.*

The car descended to the island where roads quickly became no more than oyster shell and sand. There were no high-rise condominiums for the rich or casinos for the poor to lose their government checks in. Only sea, sand and the community of those hoping and trusting to enjoy one another.

In the warmth of May, the heat only played with those who strolled the beach. Those in love who would gather a small shell, look at it and show it to their partner before casting it away. Soon the day would become twilight and the full moon would rise above the dunes, sea oats and waves. The sound of summer's laughter could be heard as they drove along the narrow road towards their sea cottage.

Nancy looked at Max. "I wonder what happened to Sea Dreams. It was so many years ago that I have forgotten on what street it was located. I know that storms have come to St. George and many of the older dwellings have been destroyed, or at least I think so."

Suddenly, Sea Dreams, appeared before them just as it had twenty years earlier when they were young and very much in love. It faced the sea just as it had on their first arrival. The wood was altered by decades of sun and storms.

"It doesn't look occupied. Do you think the agent would allow us to change houses? They are listed by the same real estate company."

"Heavens, what on earth for? All I see is twenty years of neglect," said Max sternly.

"I am not talking about our relationship but about Sea Dreams," Nancy said seriously.

"Okay, go ahead and make a mistake," said Max as he turned the car around and headed towards Gulf State Realty.

It was not a difficult transaction to make since Sea Dreams was vacant and the real estate agent was more than happy to not refund the deposit that they had made on the other large house that sat in a gated community of the privileged. As the real estate agent handed them the key, he wondered why they wanted such an old cottage when they were obviously people of wealth.

They drove in silence. Nancy looking at the blowing sea oats lining the narrow road that led to the house. Max stared straight ahead in order to avoid any eye contact with her. He felt offended that she had not taken the hint that he had offered to not change houses. To him a house was a status symbol. It was never a home but a place to entertain important people and to impress anyone driving by. What if someone important were to see his car parked in front of such a plain-Jane house?

They entered the beach sand and oyster road that led to the sea cottage. It had retained its name despite all the years: Sea Dreams. They both loved the name even though other cottages adopted the same title later on.

Then suddenly Sea Dreams appeared as though emerging from a photograph taken so long ago. Sand dunes grasped the pilings that it sat upon just as they had so many years ago. The hurricane shutters had been painted a deep green and glistened in the bright sun. For a moment, he felt relieved that it had not changed. He needed the comfort of the familiar at that moment.

Nancy stared motionless at the house for the first time in twenty years. Within her mind, she could see her son playing in the sand and then running to enter the shallow surf, claiming to have found a sand dollar when only a fragment existed within his small hand. Into his bucket, he placed the shells whose beauty existed only along the shoreline.

The house had not aged well. Its rough wood exterior no longer held the white paint that they remembered. The steps leading to the cottage were loose and rickety. They stood on the front deck before entering, the wind blowing through their hair. They looked seaward and for a brief moment were young and very much in love again.

THE PORCH FACED THE SEA JUST AS IT HAD when Max cooked hot dogs on the wooden porch. In the evenings, he would look at the stars through his telescope. Nancy often wondered what he thought as he peered at galaxies so far away. What did he see that he failed to share with her? Hours spent looking into a world that he alone shared with the stars. Perhaps it was isolation from her that he sought within the lens.

No, he loved me then. I know that he did! she thought.

She remembered how the cool damp sand in the early morning hours felt good under their feet. The moments that she cherished the most were their long walks along the beach at twilight when the moon gently touched the incoming swells and the surf whispered to them. The setting sun felt warm upon her bare shoulders, the sand warm beneath her feet.

He had loved her then, before he made his fortune; before the long moments away from her; before the affairs that were to consume his evenings. She guessed that every woman felt that moment of separation. Perhaps it occurred when the freshness of youth was lost, the moment when desire vanished from the heart.

In silence, they exited the car. Max first carried his heavy suitcases, placing them on the wooden porch steps. Then he returned to the car and took her luggage up the steep steps, breathing heavily as he ascended.

Max undid the lock and slid the door open. The rooms smelt of decaying carpet and rubber mattresses.

Besides the sounds of the breakers and seagulls, a wind chime sounded beautiful cords in the dying mid-afternoon breeze. Nancy unloaded the groceries and began to rearrange the light bamboo furniture the way she remembered it. A small couch was placed before the porch doors so that they could later sit and look beyond the sea oats and sand dunes towards the sea and coastal clouds.

Upon his entering the large, eclectically adorned room, he paused and starred at the sea-worn furnishings. A large wicker couch with a seashell pattern resided against the plywood paneling, a dark-colored synthetic wood deeply scratched by strangers. The other walls were off-white, a color likely produced by latent cigarette smoke more so than the proper mixing of chemicals. He cut on the overhead paddle fan, its blades slowly rotating in competition with the sea breeze that entered through the opened door.

Nancy immediately opened all the windows. Soon the house filled with the odors of the sea. To her, it was the rebirth of a dream until now kept silent within her thoughts.

Max reached down to cut on one of the two seashell lamps, but the bulb had burned out. Instantly, Max felt frustrated that Nancy's decision was based solely on nostalgia. "Why must we relive the past?" he asked as he stood in the doorway.

She did not reply.

Max then entered and placed the two large suitcases on the scarred pine floor of the cottage. He removed his shoes reluctantly but the remembrance of the sandy floor of the past created a strong feeling within him. The cool floor felt good as he stretched himself out on the sofa.

They sat silently, waiting for the other to speak.

"Nancy, what do we do next?" he asked.

She did not understand the depth of his question. Was he asking about the present or the future? "I do not know," she replied uneasily.

After unpacking their things, Max sat down beside her on the couch that faced the sea. They remained silent for a brief moment.

"Do you still love him?" he asked.

Nancy turned towards him. "What are you talking about? Love who?"

"The young man you screwed two years after we got married."

"Are you kidding? You think I loved him? He was just a mere infatuation, nothing more." Nancy thought that he no longer thought about her affair with another man so soon after their marriage. Max was a man who could not easily forget or forgive the past.

"Did we come here to relive the bitter past or to discover once more what made this island so beautiful to us?" she asked.

Max looked away and hesitated for a moment as he searched for an answer to her question. He knew that they both had nothing to gain by being silent or bringing up their past. At the moment, he felt tired and defenseless.

He turned towards her and, with uncustomary gentleness, asked, "Would you like to walk on the beach? The air is cool enough and the sun is lowering. I know how afraid of the sun you are. Skin cancer is not something to toy with."

Nancy looked at him. She had not expected him to want to walk on the beach with her, especially since they had just arrived and his earlier tone had been one of bitterness.

He walked over to where she was seated and took her hand. As they walked to the porch and began their descent, Max paused and closed his eyes while inhaling deeply the strong salty odors of the beach. He was afraid that if he exhaled, the dream would vanish, like so many, forever lost within the past. It was like they were young again, careless, filled with urges that could only be expressed in youth.

She wondered why he hesitated at the threshold of the sea. Max then preceded ahead of her down the steps. The warm sand felt good under their bare feet as they walked towards the sea. Soon the sand turned cool as their feet splashed into the oncoming rivulets of the small basin of sun-warmed water entrapped by the receding tide. A variety of living things – small fish, hermit crabs and other invertebrate dwellers of the shallow sea – moved in the water. At the very bottom lay a complete sand dollar. They paused looking at their reflections in the still water. He looked at her reflected image with a tenderness unfamiliar to him. He no longer wanted to fight with her or gain a victory over her. It was enough to just be there on the beach alone with her. He reached down into the pool and grasped the sand dollar in his hand. He looked at it to make sure that it was whole before placing it in Nancy's hand.

He took her other hand and together they walked down the beach. Small children appeared in the mist-filled distance, playing with a large blue-and-red beach ball. Further down the beach were surf fishermen, their rods bending with the pull of the tide and wind. They walked holding hands without speaking – the silence of a church when first entered, hushed in reverence yet keenly aware of the presence of love unseen.

In that moment of silence, thoughts were shared in a softness that words do not convey, images felt only within the heart.

As they walked, they both smiled, not at one another, but a smile seen only by the sand and driftwood of the beach. The color of the light soon changed its hue. The clouds became multicolored warm pastels of twilight. Large clouds seemed to rise from the sea and extend into the heavens. Nancy sat down on the sand and folded her legs beneath her, placing her hands behind her buttocks, her legs tight together. The dying breeze wove through her hair.

They did not speak as the moon rose over the Gulf of Mexico. The moon was a palette of changing colors as it ascended – from the silver color of daylight to the passionate red of twilight. Perhaps deep within the bosom of the sea-born cloud, thunder roared but was not seen that evening upon the beach.

The sea only whispered as the scent of salt and tide intensified with the passing of the sun. Nancy placed her hand on the sand close to Max hoping that he would touch hers. She drew a small heart with her index finger, then quickly erased it with the sweep of her palm.

He was keenly aware of her gesture. In many ways he wanted to embrace her and to make passionate love. Yet he hesitated for a reason that he did not know. He sat motionless on the damp sand. Nancy stood up feeling rejected by his indifference. She felt the warmth of the dying breeze, alone within herself, yet she longed for him. To have him within her, to share everything that love and life offered. She knew how foolish it was to waste life, that brief time wherein everyone exist. Too soon no trace would be found.

They started to walk back to the sea cottage – not touching, not understanding their own emotions, alone within themselves. Were they not free to make love as they had in college when every day was filled with smiles and the present was the future?

Like Nancy, Max remembered when they first saw the sea cottage. How they swam nude in the ocean under the Milky Way, the only source of light except for the distance glimmer of fishermen's lanterns and a few campfires, the source of distant laughter. He remembered them making love and then holding Nancy tightly in his arms until the light played once more upon the ocean.

He loved to awaken first and look at her lying there upon the many cottage pillows, locked within a feathery embrace. He could not believe how beautiful she was to him. Why does beauty once created not remain like the paintings of an artist? Is it not the same sea, the same morning sun, the red twilight that he sees even now?

As they walked, Nancy thought of all the wasted moments, the arguments, the threats of a divorce. She loved him too much to leave him yet she ached for the intimacy of love, the understanding and nurturing that can exist.

THEY SAT IN SEPARATE CHAIRS, bright indifferent reading lamps providing the illumination. Outside the wind blew strongly, moving the sea oats in swirling motions like dancers swaying. They did not speak as they read. She was reading a contemporary novel while he struggled once more to read *Ulysses*. He had only read excerpts before in preparation for her test when they first met. He had promised himself that someday he would finish it. It was like a challenge to him even though he was too restless to digest the meaning hidden within a wealth of symbolic images. He was entertained and agitated by the complexity of Joyce's writing.

"Nancy, did you bring the Guinness that I asked you to buy

last week?"

"Max, don't worry, you can have your beer when you want it. Just tell me and I will get a bottle for you." Max felt that it was necessary to drink only the beer of his ancestral land. Anything else detracted from his culture and acted as a statement of defeat. He wished inwardly that he were pure Irish like his grandmother. When referring to his father's side of the family, he was fond of saying that the English dogs had diluted the bloodline. For some reason, he felt that the English were the cause of all the misfortune that had occurred to Ireland. His grandmother had been more than willing to agree with him.

"Yes, that would be nice," he replied. "Don't forget to put two ice cubes in it." After being homeported in the Far East, he had gotten used to putting ice cubes in his beer as was the custom of those who ventured into the Orient of the past.

Nancy obediently got up from her chair and opened the refrigerator in search of his symbolic family crest, the Celtic harp upon a bottle of Guinness, the obligatory expression of a lost culture that resided now only within the stories created by the gifted. The Irish majority, the poor having been without literary voice.

Max, though not admitting it to others, found Yeats' works to be as difficult to read as those of Joyce. "Why can't Irish writers just be normal?" he often muttered to himself. He felt that even the late Poet Laureate of Ireland, Seamus Heaney, had written not for the masses but for the intellectual few who pretended to understand. "Give me a Rod McKuen any day of the week. At least that is a person I can understand."

Outside, the wind blew stronger. A beach chair skidded across the wooden deck as a gust lifted its canvas. Max arose and walked out onto the deck. He stood looking at the clear night sky. The stars were of different colors but all were clear and brilliant. He thought back to his numerous affairs and then thought only of Nancy.

WHILE MAX WAS AWAY on one of his frequent business trips, Nancy had decided to enroll at the local university. The campus was close by, eliminating the need for a lengthy commute. She decided to enroll in a graduate art class. She was a fairly accomplished artist yet without a showing.

Her professor exuded magnetism as he maintained eye contact while offering a criticism of her work. As he spoke about hues and texture, he smiled. It was obvious to her that he was flirting.

As the semester progressed, he would lightly touch her shoulder while examining her work. He compared her paintings to Henri Matisse. Her use of color was exceptional, her artistic designs fascinating. He felt that her nudes expressed unrepentant sexuality.

"Ms. Shell, as you know I really have grown to appreciate your work. I think that you of all of my students should have a showing." The university maintained a small gallery in the city. Every art student sought to have their work shown publicly. Even if it resulted in bitter criticism, at least they had a showing. A clipping in the paper that announced the event. Now Nancy had been chosen to be so complimented.

"Dr. Leland, I am honored that you have chosen me. As you know, I want to develop as an artist. As an artist, I must learn to accept public criticism."

"You have a great deal of potential," he said as he peered into her eyes. He was tall with wavy black hair and wore a smile that drew women into his spire of erotic desire. Her body felt his presence more than her mind. It was the attraction that the moon must force upon the ocean. She had neither will nor power to withdraw from his presence. "I would like to discuss your work at greater detail in my office tonight." Max was out of town on business for several days. That night she felt very alone, defenseless in her loneliness.

"Thank you for taking a personal interest in my work," she said with a smile.

"I always want to motivate my students to work harder on their projects. Art demands more than the stroke of the brush. An artist must be a promoter as well as having some basic talent. There are plenty artists that just mimic what they see. They paint like photographers. What good is that? You might as well have a camera. You must see within the subject to be a great artist. Art, unlike that which is written, can go beyond the limitations of words. Language is too limited in the expression of emotions. There is no limit in the world of the painter."

She looked at him. "I want to find that world that you are describing, to exceed the limits of written language."

She followed him down the dimly lit hallway to his office. It was a small room with table lamps instead of the usual florescent tubes so common in academia. The rich wood of the office and the two leather chairs for student appointments lent a gentleman's club ambience.

He turned towards her. "I will help you find the ability to create beyond verbal expression." As he spoke, he put his arms around her and drew her closer to him. She did not resist but instead began to undo his shirt and then his trousers. He took her that evening as a man takes a woman, unafraid.

She wanted to flee from his desire but could not.

AS THEIR AFFAIR CONTINUED, STUDENTS COULD OVERHEAR faculty members as they discussed the inappropriate relationship. It was not long until Max knew of her unfaithfulness. It would have ended their marriage except for the guilt that he felt himself. He reasoned that since he had affairs, she was entitled to her own as long as they did not cost him money or time. To Max, time was the most important commodity of all.

If she left him, he knew that he would be able to make up the financial loss. He would be free of her. But then he wondered what freedom was. Free for what? To make more money, to seduce another woman?

Nancy's affair soon ended when she discovered that her lover was having multiple relationships at the same time. When she asked Professor Leland to see only her, he laughed, as would a man who felt that she was totally replaceable. Even though he was fascinated by her wealth, he was not interested in a relationship that required fidelity. Nancy was no more special to him than any other student that he was having an affair with. His relationship with her was one of desire, not love.

From the time Max discovered her infidelity, they no longer slept together. He resented, yet understood her.

THAT NIGHT WITH THE SEA WIND BLOWING, Nancy said, "Max, would you like to hold me? Perhaps even to kiss me?" She did not look at him as she spoke.

He was taken aback by her question. It had been years since he had shown any affection towards her. Max felt more repulsion than attraction. For a moment, he did not reply. Then he looked firmly at her. "For what reason?"

She did not answer but continued reading. Outside a mist was forming along the beach as the sea oats and pines moved to the symphony of wind.

MAX AWOKE TO THE AROMA of freshly ground Boston Harbor coffee. The aroma always stirred memories in him. With his family being Irish, they enjoyed black morning tea made more palatable with cream, sugar and a morning cookie. It was in the Navy that he learned to drink coffee in order to stay awake on the long watches required of those who served on destroyers. Later as he pursued his graduate degrees, coffee kept him alert and responsive even during the midnight hours required of a Harvard MBA student.

He walked barefoot into the kitchen and found Nancy preparing eggs and bacon – his favorites. Her kind smile disarmed him as did the rich odors in the kitchen. He had intended not to speak to her, but that was now impossible.

"Good morning," he said softly.

"Good morning," she replied without looking in his direction. She was wearing her short cream-colored pajamas covered by a light green gown that moved with the sea wind. She looked beautiful to him yet he could not express it. He wanted to press her tightly against his bare chest and tell her that he loved her, but could not. Deep down he felt that it was too late to love her. He felt that his love for her could not return yet he desired it.

He looked at the firmness of her breasts and the round contours of her buttocks, then looked away for he did not want her to be aware of his desire. Should she notice, it would be a defeat for his ego. Yet he could not help but look at the flowing gown made translucent in the awakening sun.

"Max, after we eat, would you enjoy driving into Apalachicola?" she asked in an almost apologetic tone.

At first, he wanted to say, "What for?" After a pause, he said instead, "Yes, that would be nice. You and I have not walked along the wharf since we were young college students. I would enjoy that." He remembered how joyful they were when they first drove into the small fishing village. Full of hope and desire for what must surely lie ahead for them. Perhaps it was only the dream that came from youth when everything was possible, a time to exist in the moment of each other.

THEY PARKED NEAR THE DOCK. The strong smell of diesel from the fishing vessels, when mixed with the salty air, added a sea aroma like that of Galveston. He checked each door of the Land Rover to make sure that it was securely locked against thieves. Then they walked as strangers do, apart and unaware of each other.

"Max, there are so many new shops," she said with a brief glance in his direction.

"Why don't we go separate ways? There is a nautical shop that features salvaged marine items that I would like to visit," he said. She did not acknowledge his suggestion but quickly entered the Sea Hatter boutique shop.

Max continued to walk down the sparsely populated sidewalk on his way to the salvage shop. He noticed the women in their sundresses, bare shoulders and barely supported breasts.

One particularly attractive woman smiled at him. As he continued to walk, he turned back to look at her. He noticed that she entered a bar named THE CATCH OF THE DAY. He was not in a hurry and thought, *Why not?*

He immediately turned around and approached the bar. Loud country and western music guided him to the entrance. Before entering, the smell of alcohol, beer and cigarettes greeted him as a hostess might have in the Far East. It took a moment for his eyes to adjust to the dim light of the interior. A large bald man with thick tattooed arms stood behind the bar guarding the bottles. Other than the bartender, the room seemed empty.

Max stood there for a moment in silence. As awkwardness overtook him, he said, "I will have a Corona draft."

"We don't have that on tap," said the bartender, obviously offended at the request.

"I will have whatever you do have on tap," replied Max, as he looked once more around the empty room. "Didn't I see a young woman enter here just a moment ago?"

"Maybe you did," replied the keeper of bottles.

Max walked over to a table and sat down. After tasting the cold liquid intoxicant, he felt a tap on his shoulder.

"You looking for me?" asked the woman that had smiled at him on the sidewalk.

"Yes, I suppose I am," he replied with an awkward smile.

"Well, whoever you are, you found me," she said.

"May I buy you a beer?" he asked speaking loudly above the music.

"You can when I get off work," she said as she raised her dress in order to massage her tanned thigh, revealing a most unusual tattoo: two islands joined by a gold coin. The coin had a jade dragon within it.

"I am sorry, I didn't know you were a hostess here."

She laughed. "Is that what they call it?"

"Yes, I will call it that," he said, looking into her cobalt blue eyes.

"Call it what you will. I don't get off until one in the morning. Is that too late for a mature man?" she said seriously.

"Since you have accepted my invitation. I imagine that we need to exchange names," said Max with a broad smile.

"What for?" she asked seriously.

"Can I just call you Thing?" said Max, laughing.

"Thing will do and I will call you It."

"It and Thing. It sounds like we are in a jungle movie," he replied. "Then grunts will fit in just fine." He did not know what to think of her. She was beautiful in a crude way with her dyed blond ponytail and dark spray-on tan. He also had observed the blue jean miniskirt that revealed her legs and accented her figure. As she placed his beer on the table, she bent forward revealing what he assumed to be augmented breasts. Yet, even with her crudeness, she fascinated him.

"Is it possible that you might be able to get off work a little earlier?"

"Does your wife always require you to have affairs early in the evening?"

"One in the morning will be just fine. Do I pick you up here at the bar or do we meet at your place?"

"My place. I have a cabin on the water. Let's first meet at the city dock. I will drive us there."

"You must make a lot of money as a hostess," he said, checking whether she was serious or not.

"No, I make very little. My husband wanted to fish more than he wanted to make love. He bought the cabin while serving in Afghanistan."

"Where is he now?"

"He was killed there. He left me the cabin, a government pension and debt."

"Okay, all I have to do is find the city dock and meet you there after one."

"Finish your beer and get some sleep. Besides, I am sure that by now your wife has spent enough money."

Max was not used to having anyone give him a command. At first, he was angry but then he reasoned that an argument with a stranger would prove of no value to him. "See you then."

HE REENTERED THE STREET. It was warm, causing light sweat to form on his brow. He reached into his pocket and retrieved his cell phone. He dialed it and spoke softly, "Nancy, are you just about finished with your shopping? If so, let's meet at the Gypsy Girl and have a beer before returning to Sea Dreams."

Nancy, who was used to receiving orders, wondered why he was being so nice to her. She knew that he was going to be very displeased with the amount of money that she had spent. She desperately wanted to look attractive for him so cost was not an issue. Equifax had already alerted him of the decrease in his Gold Card. Rather than the amount that she had spent, he was usually more concerned about having to carry the items afterwards.

She was aware that he was attracted to other women but she thought that here in Apalachicola wonderful memories might return to him and things could possibly become okay between them.

THEY WALKED TOWARDS THE GYPSY GIRL, crossing the oyster-and-sea-sand path that led to the inn. It was an inn that faced the Apalachicola River. When they had first arrived in the port village, they had spent their first night there. Nancy remembered the boat traffic that tied up to the inn at night. Noises of diesel engines, boats hitting the wharf that adjoined their room. At times she had thought she could feel the room move from their collisions.

The bar was built on a small wharf that extended beyond the inn. There they sat down and looked at the menu. She ordered the house red wine while he requested a Guinness from the red-headed waitress.

"Let's have some Apalachicola oysters," he said, looking up at the waitress. "Not that I need them."

The waitress did not react to his comment but instead jotted down the order and quickly vanished into the darkness of the inn.

"Must you flirt with every woman that you meet? I don't object, really I don't, as long as you do it behind my back. I don't want to look abused in front of others."

Max did not reply but instead sipped his beer while looking at the aftermath of a large splash upon the surface of the river. "The mackerel must be running," he said authoritatively. It was as though they inhabited two different worlds. He increasingly failed to acknowledge her presence.

She wondered how love could flee so totally. The warm wind blew from off the tall sea grass mixing with the odors of the river and bar. *If only today could be yesterday. If only he would touch me again.*

"May I get you another beer?" said the waitress once he had drained his glass.

"No, one beer will do me." He then looked at Nancy. "Hun, will you have another glass of wine?"

"Yes, I will. Thank you."

They sat there by the river. He wanted her to drink as never before. He wanted her to drink so much that she would fall asleep immediately upon their return to the sea cottage. That way he would not have to prepare such an elaborate lie for leaving her at one o'clock in the morning.

THE SETTING SUN TURNED RED AS IT NEARED THE WATERS OF THE BAY. Nancy rested her head against the car window as Max drove across the causeway. Their lack of conversation was not unusual. Silence was an easy companion to have.

Upon arriving at Sea Dreams, Nancy entered the cabin while Max positioned a beach chair on the porch. He admired that she was able to drink so much without staggering. He knew that she would soon be asleep on the couch. Since she took sedatives, she should sleep very soundly. He only wished that he could go to the dock sooner. He felt full of energy and desire.

Max watched a large schooner slicing through the summer waves. The wind cooled him while the setting sun cast warmth upon the porch. He felt a great deal of anticipation as he awaited the opportunity to return Apalachicola where he had arranged a meeting with the attractive stranger.

What is in it for her? I am not an unattractive man and I am still reasonably young, but so are many men that stroll along the streets of Apalachicola. Perhaps she is nothing more than a common prostitute. I will not lower myself to pay for sex. I hope that she just wants a little adventure and would like to party after she gets off work. That would satisfy me.

He smiled to himself at that last thought.

Seagulls swooped down to the beach and rode the currents of air that then lifted them back to the sky. Out on the ocean, the edge of the moon was just appearing. He looked at his Blackberry. His aunt had just sent him an attachment of his uncle's ninetieth birthday. How happy the people in the photograph appeared. All of his cousins smiling at the camera, a strong feeling of family bond. In truth Max envied them. They had found what they were looking for – children, jobs that satisfied them and, most importantly, they had found someone to love.

Soon the darkness overpowered the twilight. The moon ascended in its brightness. Max was hardly aware of the passage of time. He looked through the window at Nancy who lay on the seashell-patterned couch. He arose and gently opened the screen door. Then for a reason unknown to him, he took a blanket from the bedroom and covered her. She looked so young lying there. He thought of all of the wonderful moments that they had shared in Sea

Dreams. The laughter, the lovemaking, the caring they had for each another. For a moment, he experienced an emotion deep within, an overwhelming sense of loss.

AS HE DROVE BACK OVER THE CAUSEWAY, HE FELT CONFUSED. He was leaving behind a person that had loved him with all of her heart. Now he was driving towards the arms of a stranger who would almost certainly want something from him. Her desire for him was too easy, too staged.

He soon drove down the wharf and parked near a streetlight about which insects flew aimlessly. It was already ten past one as he waited. Then he saw a car approaching. His heart pounded with both dread and anticipation. The car pulled in next to him. He could see the outline of her face. She did not say anything. He opened his door and approached the passenger side of the car.

"Good to see you," he said, climbing into her car. She did not reply but instead lit a cigarette and put the car in reverse. She then quickly shifted into drive as the car sped over the ground swells of the road.

Still without a word, she turned onto a narrow oyster road that led into the thickness of the underbrush. Large palms and pines lined the road as she sped along, her cigarette glowing in the darkness of the car.

"You do live in a remote area. Have you lived here long?" he said as he looked at her exposed knees illuminated by the dials of the car.

"Long enough," she replied.

"Married, divorced, single? Oh yes, widowed. How foolish of me to have forgotten. I guess that covers just about every category. I must assume that you have a boyfriend that works somewhere around here.

She remained silent as she made a right turn into a driveway. Max could make out the shape of a two-story house that faced a lagoon. An owl called from the trees. She opened her door and stepped out into the night. The moonlight revealed her form. Max opened his door as well and joined her in front of the car. Then she opened the door of the cottage without inserting a key.

"You must either trust people or you forgot and left your house unlocked."

"I have good neighbors," she said, cutting the light switch on.

To Max's surprise, a bearded man was sitting in a chair holding a double-barreled shotgun in his lap. "Well stranger, you are a welcome sight indeed. You must have thought that Lorrie-Lynn was one sure thing," he said as he smiled at her.

Lorrie-Lynn walked over to where the man was seated and placed her hand on his shoulder.

"What is going on here?" asked Max who could hear his own heart beating in his chest.

"What do you think is going on here, asshole?" asked the man mockingly.

Max regained his composure as well as his anger. "Listen, friend, I must assume that you want something from me such as my wallet, money or ring."

"Lorrie-Lynn, he is one smart asshole. He sounds like one of those college-educated type. The kind that thinks they know something but don't know shit," he said with a laugh. "Let's start with you handing Lorrie your shirt and trousers just like you had planned on doing. The only thing different is that you have extra company. Does that bother you any?"

Without replying, Max removed his shirt and trousers and handed them to her. She remained silent as she took them and placed them in a sack.

"Now take off your socks, shorts and shoes. Some sons of bitches hide their money in their sock or in the bottom of their shoe. Just can't be too careful when taking someone's pride and joy – his money."

For the first time in his life, Max did not feel self-conscious being nude before strangers. His anger grew more intense in his humiliation.

"Now I know that it is embarrassing for you to not be attired in the fashion that you are used to, polo shirt and all."

Max stared at him for the first time. He was a small built man with thinning black hair that formed a widow's peak. His beady eyes squinted the way a very nearsighted person would. His T-shirt had holes in it that made the word NIRVANA difficult to read. The trousers were faded blue denim held in place by a wide leather belt with a brass cactus belt buckle.

"I hope that you don't mind, but you and I need to walk down to the bayou and look at the moon together. Now don't get your hopes up, I only like women but a man can get used to other things while serving time. After you." He pointed to the door. Max could smell the strong odor of whiskey on his breath, which explained why he had a difficult time rising from the overstuffed chair.

Max could feel the twin barrels of the gun in his kidney. It was obvious that they planned on killing him. Why else would they have bagged his clothing? No one would ever find his blood or any trace of him in the house. He assumed that once dead, the killers would row him into the bayou, weigh him down and leave his body for the alligators and mud cats.

Max looked back. "It is not smart killing a man on your own property."

"Who says I am smart? But I am one hell of a lot smarter than you. Look whose got a gun at his back."

At that moment, a vehicle's headlights could be seen turning into the long, winding drive. Lorrie-Lynn shouted, "Marci, we got company."

He turned towards her and shouted, "Yow, I seen the car. Looks like the asshole may have some company tonight."

With Marci's back turned towards him, Max jumped from the pier into the water just as the shotgun discharged. Luckily, the range was so close that the buckshot did not have the opportunity to spread its killing force. Max dove straight to the bottom and kicked with all of his might parallel to the shore, using a slimy cypress stump for cover.

Max heard another burst of gunfire and then it was silent. He did not know if the gunfire was directed at him or at the vehicle entering the driveway. It did not matter; he was alive and filled with adrenalin. Luckily, he had been trained in the Navy to swim lengthy distances in ink-black water, surfacing only to get a new bearing from the moon.

Emerging from the swamp, his feet sank into the mud of collective years of swamp growth and death. He quickly found a road and began to run down it. He did not know what direction to run but he ran even faster hoping to find a house, fishermen or any place of refuge. A few pellets of buckshot had penetrated his buttocks and he was bleeding. He realized that being naked and covered with mud and blood would frighten anyone that saw him. He would just have to take his chances. The more he ran, the deeper the new lacerations on his feet hurt, but he ignored the pain. In his haste, he did not feel a piece of broken whiskey bottle in the soft dust of the road pierce his skin.

Running, running was all he could do. An SUV approached him. He stood in the middle of the road. Soon blue lights above the vehicle flashed on.

"Stand right where you are and keep your arms high in the air," shouted a voice. He saw a form approach him. The unknown person grabbed his arms and handcuffed him from behind.

"What the hell are you doing running down a county road without your pants on? Drugs?" asked the officer.

"No sir, my name is Maximillian Shell, and I have just escaped from, in all probability, being murdered."

"You obviously don't have any identification on you." The officer laughed. "We will go to town and have you formally booked for indecent exposure to start with. I will also get a urine sample from you. You don't smell of alcohol, but we need to check for drugs just the same."

In the light of the car, the officer could see blood oozing from his backside and feet. "I hope you are not HIV positive. We have a hospital in town but no doctors. There is a nurse there, or at least she is supposed to be there. Sally can stop the bleeding and, if need be, we will call a chopper to airlift you out to a real hospital. I will call in and have her waiting on us."

THEY APPROACHED THE HOSPITAL, a one-story 1950s looking building of cinder block construction. Upon their arrival, a small woman with a sweater approached the SUV.

"Got a bleeder here, Sally. He claims that someone was trying to kill him. From all the blood, I think that they came very close to doing just that."

Sally gave Max a hospital gown and surgical socks that clung to the blood and irritated the wounds even further. After putting the gown and socks on, he was handcuffed again. "Yep, Fred, this is buckshot. The only question is why anyone would try to shoot him at three in the morning. There has been some talk about a voyeur peeking into houses around here. Probably got shot looking into someone's bedroom."

"He must think himself quite a lover." Fred laughed.

"I swear, my name is Max Shell, and I am wealthy. I can pay to look at a woman. I don't need a bathroom window to peer into."

"Sally, does he look wealthy to you?" Fred laughed. "Can you get the buckshot out or do we need to medevac him to Tallahassee? First, we need to take some pictures of his ass."

"Oh, I almost forgot," she replied. She went to the cabinet and produced a digital camera with a macro lens. After taking several shots of his buttocks and the soles of his feet, she said, "I can get the shot out." She then looked at Max. "How is your tolerance for pain?"

"I can take it, but please let me have whatever drug you have to make it less painful."

She handed him a Valium that she took from her purse and a glass of water.

"Is that all that you have?" he asked. Sally looked at Fred and smiled.

Max felt the probe go deep into his hip. "What the fuck!" he yelled in pain. "Oh, that hurts. Damn it, woman!"

"Come on, sailor. Since you may be facing some time in the slammer, you need to get used to being penetrated," Fred said with a chuckle.

When Sally finished, she sutured the wounds and Fred handcuffed him again.

"Is it standard procedure to handcuff a man who has just had surgery?" asked Max.

Fred looked at the nurse. "Sally, I need to make a few phone calls. Would you object to sitting with him for a couple of minutes? He is too much of a wimp to cause you too much trouble. If he does, just hit him with something on the ass."

"You two must think that this is pretty funny," Max said as he glared at Sally. "You won't find it so funny after I make my allotted call to my New York lawyer."

"Where are going to get the fifty cents needed to make a call? Oh, I forgot, Fred will loan you the money. Like hell he will! If you go talking 'lawyers,' he may just put you back in the swamp. If I was you, I would treat him real nice."

Several minutes passed before Fred returned.

"I called Edna at Sea Coast Realty. Her company manages the rentals on the road where we picked him up. Seems that none of them are rented. If any of them was broken into, we can charge him for breaking and entering. I will go ahead and take him to the slammer and let him make his allotted call. Then we will see what the district attorney has in mind."

Max said softly, almost confidentially, "This is a little awkward for me. You see, I have a wife waiting for me on St. George Island. Is there a way we can settle this without her getting involved?"

"First, you know that it is a violation of the law to offer a sheriff's deputy a bribe. We may be rural America but we are honest folks. I will just pretend that you didn't say what you just did. Do you agree, Sally, or did you hear this Yankee offer me a bribe?"

"Well, Fred, since he has been nice enough, I guess my ears have been too stopped-up to hear anything."

Fred once more removed the handcuffs. "Get your pants on. Oh, I forgot, you don't have any. Sally, get him some clothes from the charity drop locker."

ON THE TWENTY-MINUTE DRIVE TO THE COURTHOUSE, Max tried to rationalize what had happened to him. At the same time, he was thankful to be alive. Should he just admit to Nancy everything that had happened that evening – make a clean sweep of his mistake – or should he try to fabricate a lie? Max was not a good liar. Whenever he was caught in an awkward situation, he just chose to say nothing. This time, however, he could not remain silent. He knew that the man and woman who had kidnapped him had, in all probability, done this before. They needed to be stopped. Since they had taken his wallet and cell phone, he realized that he was in danger since they could later, if they desired, trace his every move.

Upon arrival at the county courthouse, he was booked and led into what appeared to be an interrogation room. As soon they sat him down, the balding, overweight district attorney entered, wiping sweat off his brow.

"I don't know why in the world they always paint the windows shut. If you are going to hire incompetent painters, at least keep the air-conditioning fixed," he said without looking at Max. Obviously his comments were intended only for himself. At that point, he read Max his rights for the second time. "Now tell me again what happened."

Max repeated the story of the abduction and attempted murder.

The district attorney looked at him. "Tell me what those two characters looked like."

Afterwards Max was brought into a nondescript room and left sitting in a hard wooden chair. His buttocks ached as he waited not knowing what to expect. He sat there in silence until an officer arrived with a drunk who was then seated across from him.

"Well, Professor, what you in for?" asked the newly arrived prisoner.

"Uh, I am in here because no one will listen to me," Max replied uneasily.

"Same with me. Ain't a shit ass that will give me the time of day. I want to know what is wrong with a man taking a drink in public. I bet that the shit ass that arrested me is doing a lot worse things to his wife and dog. Ain't a dick in Appalach that can cast a stone. No sir, not one." He then sat there silent as though waiting for an appointment. Soon he was uttering loud snores that Max found himself counting.

"Mr. Shell, follow me!" a voice said from the doorway. Max followed obediently. "Have you been read your rights? Have you been given the opportunity to make a phone call?" The short, overweight policewoman smelled strongly of Walmart-purchased perfume.

"Yes, I have been read my rights, but I have not been given an opportunity to make a phone call."

"Use the phone on the desk and limit the call to five minutes or less," said the policewoman who obviously enjoyed her position over prisoners.

Max picked up the receiver and tried to remember his lawyer's phone number. Unfortunately, he could not remember the number. He knew that time was passing on his five minutes. Finally, he decided to call Nancy. The phone rang her number several times and then went to voice mail.

"I cannot believe she is not picking up. Surely she is worried about me," he muttered. Suddenly the door opened and Nancy entered the room accompanied by a police officer.

"Your wife wants to talk to you," the policeman said loudly as he remained within listening distance.

"Nancy, what are you doing here?"

"When I awoke, you were gone. No note, no call, nothing. I remembered how you used to take a morning swim far out in the ocean before breakfast. I was afraid that you had been caught in a rip tide. That is when I called the police. They said that they have arrested you on a breaking and entering charge. What on earth are you doing in here?"

"I was kidnapped and taken to a remote location. I barely escaped with my life."

"I don't understand. You were kidnapped? How on earth did that happen?"

"Just take my word for it," Max said with an unfamiliar tone of defeat.

THE POLICEWOMAN HAD IN THE MEANTIME RECEIVED a call on another line.

"Mr. Shell, follow me." She led him to a large courtroom where the local judge was seated. The room smelt of old documents intensified by the closed windows that had also been painted shut. Nancy followed them slowly as though she were a reluctant visitor to a proceeding that she wanted no part of.

The judge looked at him with a degree of curiosity. "Mr. Shell, we don't often see a man with your background in my court. Edna, the lady who manages the homes along the bayou where you were arrested checked on each of the houses. Magic Lagoon has been broken into. Officer Fred Scout has already told me about the incident. I must say I can't believe that you fell for such a scam. You could have lost your life. What makes me think that you are innocent is that this same thing happened to another gentleman. I tell you what, if you are willing to pay the cost of damages as determined by Edna, let's see"—he thumbed through a stack of paper—"that is five thousand dollars, then I am willing to dismiss the case. You will also have to pay court cost."

"Your honor, five thousand dollars! I have done nothing wrong!" Max said loudly barely able to control his emotions.

"Your wife will have to be the one to rule on that," the judge said as he looked down at Nancy.

Max once more addressed the judge, "It was another fellow called Marci that broke in. Not me!"

The judge looked at him. "You really are a lucky man. All you are worried about is money and from what I understand, you have plenty of it." He paused for just a moment. "A junior college student and his girlfriend had just pulled into the driveway of Magic Lagoon with the intention of making out when a fellow opens fire on them. Could have killed them both had they been closer. Instead, his shotgun just scared them. He must have forgotten that he didn't have a rifle." The judge paused. "That is the only reason I am letting you go."

NANCY GLANCED AT MAX AS THEY DROVE OVER THE BRIDGE that connected Apalachicola to the mainland. "Tell me what happened. Did someone approach you on the beach and force you to go into town?"

"No, damn it. I was restless after you fell asleep on the coach. I just went to Appalach to get a drink. That's all. Just a drink."

"Max, you are a lucky man in many ways and a very foolish one in others," she said softly as though she too were his judge that day.

"I know," he said apologetically.

From the tone of his voice, she instinctually knew what had occurred. More detail from him would only penetrate deeper into her heart. "Oh, I understand. I just hope she was worth it," Nancy said as she watched a large sailboat beating to windward, its sails catching the intense light from the water and the brilliant coastal sun. Behind it were seagulls rising and falling in the wind as they waited patiently for food. Nancy felt that she too was waiting for the discards of his life. As they rode, she wondered whether she should bring up the events that led to his arrest. After all, this was a chance for her to even the mythical unwinnable score.

Nancy looked at him. "I hope that one day you will explain to me what just happened."

"Well, I can take the time now to explain," he said loudly.

Nancy screamed, "Look out! There's a fisherman standing in the road about to cast!"

"Shit," said Max as he swerved, pressing the horn. "Damn tourist!"

"Max, you too are a tourist," she responded in a teasing manner.

"Well, you don't see me standing on some fucking bridge trying to get hit!"

"No, Max, you are too gifted for that." She paused. "To think that someone is trying to have fun on a beautiful afternoon."

"What are you trying to say to me? That I don't know how to have fun?"

"Precisely! When you have what you describe to yourself as fun, someone gets hurt, especially me."

He looked sternly at her. "Don't blame your own failures on me. Don't forget that you too had an affair. How do you think that made me feel? All warm and fuzzy knowing that my wife is a classy, sophisticated slut!"

"Shut your fucking mouth and keep an eye on the road you son of a bitch!" she said loudly. Nancy knew that there was no point in talking further to him. He was never going to forgive her. It was a slave's brand that he had placed on her soul and body. She knew that she would never be free of his insults and insinuations. *Oh, he has managed to do it again – turn all the blame and fault-finding onto me as though that absolved all his sins*, she thought. *My mistakes have been few compared to his indulgences.*

THEY ARRIVED BACK AT SEA DREAMS IN SILENCE. He was not about to acknowledge the role that she had played in getting him released from the county jail, or even thank her for worrying about him.

Does he think that his whores would have given a rat's ass about him once he was in jail? Nancy thought. *Of course not.*

As he left the car, he slammed the door with a great force augmented by the wind. She stood by the car waiting for his temper to subside. She knew that ahead of her were hours of silence, but she was used to that part of her marriage.

NANCY WENT TO HER ROOM AND CLOSED THE DOOR, locking it from the inside. She lay fully dressed on the bed and watched the ceiling fan in its slow rotation.

What lies ahead for me? If I leave him, his lawyers will see to it that he gets more than his share of our possessions. He is such a coward; I know that he wants me to make the first move so he can say that I wanted a divorce. Yes, he wants me to be the villain which is so much like him. He will not care. Once he has his share of everything, I will not hear from him again. She did not know it at the time, but within her belly a new son was being formed.

Slowly twilight came, then darkness studded with starlight. The ocean whispered outside her window.

MAX LAY UNCOMFORTABLY ON HIS BED. His argument with Nancy

left him feeling exhausted.

Why argue? Wouldn't it be better if I just accepted my life as it is? he thought. "This damn room is too hot," he said out loud. Small beads of sweat ran down his forehead and entered the threads of his pillow. He arose and walked over to the row of windows that faced the beach. He unlocked the windows and attempted to raise them. They had obviously been painted shut. The more he strained, the more he sweated. "Damn it, damn it!" he shouted to the moonlight that walked ever so slowly upon the wooden planks of the porch. He felt his way to a wall switch and cut on the paddle fan. Its blades slowly rotated above his head. For a moment, the slow moving blades reminded him of the churning waters formed by the screws of the destroyer as it entered Hong Kong Bay. He once more remembered the young woman that he loved so long ago. A mere bar girl who worked in the Wan Chai district of the crowded island. She was a beautiful Eurasian of Chinese and Russian descent.

They had met when he was twenty-two and she was seventeen. He loved her more than anyone he had ever loved. It was an innocent love not driven by any hedonistic need. It was, therefore, not a relationship built on sex and power. She had nothing to give except her innocence. Hers was a smile without avarice. That was what attracted him so much to her.

The ship had just returned from gunfire support when he met her. He had left the U.S.S. *Chandler* anchored just off the main channel of Hong Kong Harbor. That evening he showered and dressed in his best casual attire. He shaved and applied a generous amount of Old Spice cologne.

The month at sea had been difficult. Days filled with shore bombardment and nights with underway replenishments in addition to harassment and interdiction fire. The enemy had to be kept awake and so did the crew of the small destroyer. He had participated in the shelling of villages and the slow methodical death of the Vietcong who manned the small gun emplacements along the beaches.

He had promised Kam that he would return for her but never did. Perhaps he never intended to.

SLOWLY HIS EYES FELT HEAVY. He got up and cut off the fan. The sound of the ocean filled the room. Soon he was asleep.

He was walking on hot sand. Mountains of red sand were about him. In the distance he could see small whirlwinds of dust. The clouds above him were the color of the sand. As he walked, he could hear women singing in a most strange accent as goatskin drums accompanied him. There on a red dune in the far distance was a solitary figure. A woman in a dark habesha kemis that flowed gracefully about her body. Her dark black hair blew in the desert wind. He was too far away to see her features except he knew that he loved her as he did Kam.

THE MORNING CAME TOO SOON. Max had no desire to leave the dream. Once more the sound of the surf entered the room and he was awake.

CHAPTER TWELVE
An Issue of Judgment

MAX JR. PICKED UP THE *NEW YORK TIMES* and began to thumb through the thick newspapers. His mother, years before, had told him repeatedly that he was a carbon copy of his late father. Max skipped the sections that did not appeal to him. As he discarded the areas he was not interested in, he noticed the travel section. Usually this area held little fascination to him, yet today his eyes fixed upon a photograph of the Pitons – the two dominant and much-photographed peaks of St. Lucia. It was the usual splash page advertisement for an all-inclusive resort. He looked closely at the Pitons, the stark images of volcanic cones that rose sharply from the Caribbean. He could not identify the strange feeling within himself. It was as though he had been there before, a different era, a different life.

He and Matthew Philips had graduated from the University of Texas together after leaving Boston College at the end of their sophomore year. They had formed a strong bond, having both received commission in the United States Navy, a family tradition in the Shell family. They graduated number one and two in their NROTC class. The fact that Matthew was number one bothered

Max, just as it would have his father, who had bequeathed to his son that number two was not good enough. Their friendship and respect for one another led to a business partnership after the obligatory service was completed.

Over the years, Matthew and Max had worked to build their diverse holdings into a major corporation that spread into a variety of fields, including petroleum, biomedical, telecom and technology. Their diversity ensured their survival when the market shifted up and down during turbulent times.

They remained competitive even though they were both leading their corporation into ever increasing stock value and sky-high profitability. The money did not matter to Max, only the stalking and the kill.

Max had met Matthew's wife at a party in the Hamptons. She was not exceptionally beautiful yet her buoyant personality made her so. She was the very opposite of Max's wife, Margaret. Gina dressed modestly yet she was sexy with her fit, trim body. Her swimming-pool tan radiated a healthy appearance.

Even though Max loved Margaret, he was bored by the repetitiveness of their relationship. She had become too predictable. They had grown apart and soon found that they had little in common during their leisure time together. There was no challenge left for Max to respond to.

As Max looked at the advertisement, he began to think of a new challenge. That of having an affair with Gina. The very idea appealed to his hunting instinct. What better way to possess Gina than to have her fall out of love with Matthew? He did not love Gina nor was he overly attracted to her. He simply wanted to be number one regardless of the contest.

What if he invited Matthew as well as other senior executives for a week in St. Lucia? He could call it a working week with a few meetings and lots of beach time. Vue de Mer would be a perfect place to stay. It was nestled between the two volcanic cones that form the Pitons. The food was reputed to be excellent and the view the best in the Caribbean.

It is an idea that appeals to my desire to hunt, thought Max. That weekend, he spent time on his computer studying the history and people of Saint Lucia. It was truly a paradise with just enough danger to make it interesting. He knew that even Eden had its serpent. Historically, it had served as a battlefield for the English and French as well as a hunting ground for the infamous marauders of the Caribbean. Deadly landslides and earthquakes had also plagued it.

The town of Soufriere sat at the base of Gros Piton, the larger of the two volcanic plugs. It had at one time been the capital city of Saint Lucia. Castries was to later assume the title. He made it a habit to always start with mundane facts before beginning any affair.

HE ARRANGED A THREE-DAY VISIT TO ST. LUCIA. It was to serve as a scouting trip to see if the locale met his needs and were not just the staging for a photo-op. On this trip, he traveled alone with only one intent. The drive to Vue de Mer from the airport was beautiful. The tropical rainforest in the tall, steep mountains wore a variety of greens. Growing wild in the volcanic soil were ylang-ylangs, African tulips, passion fruit, birds-of-paradise, bamboos and coconut palms. In the valleys were banana and coconut groves, remnants of the former great French plantations that prospered from slave labor.

Even though he was to be there for only a short time, he intended to enjoy snorkeling in the sea just off the Pitons. From his room, he could see the jungle about him, the tall Pitons before him. After purchasing the required gear, he arrived at the hotel's private beachfront area. Soon he was swimming under the warm tropical sun.

It felt so good to be in the sea that he swam further from the shore. Suddenly he was fighting a riptide that prevented him from swimming back to the beach. An unknown emotion took hold of him, that of panic. Instead of doing what he had been taught, he attempted to swim directly towards the Gros Piton. Soon his energy was depleted as he gulped salt water into his nose and mouth.

He felt something pulling him back towards the open ocean. Immediately he let himself go, following whatever force was defying his efforts. He began to drift parallel to the beach, barely treading water while trying to avoid a deadly leg cramp. As he began to sink into the clear blue-green water, he felt as though he were being lifted to the surface. Underwater, he opened his eyes. At a distance, he could see an object swimming away from him. Further and further away the entity moved until it vanished.

When he rose to the surface, the riptide had ended. Slowly he swam towards the beach. When he could touch the sand, he staggered several yards and then fell. He turned over facing the sun and lay still in the calmness of the shallow tidal pool.

That evening after having drunk two whisky sours, he rested under the protection of the mosquito net that clung to the four-poster bed. Soon he was asleep. In his dream, a woman motioned for him to enter the sea. He was unable to see her features as the wind blew her hair across her face. Soon she beckoned him into the surf. Max could feel the energy of the waves as they lifted him. No matter how fast he swam, he could not reach her. He swam further and further away from the shore but it did not matter to him.

He awoke as the sun entered his room. At first, he could not tell what was real as the dream clung to his awakened thoughts. Regardless of the questions swirling in his mind, he felt comforted by the mountains and sea of the small island of St. Lucia.

ON HIS RETURN TO HIS HOUSE IN CONNECTICUT, a home that he had inherited from his father, Max leaned back in his leather chair and looked upon the green pastures, manicured for his afternoon golf. He poured himself a whiskey, dropped a cherry in it, and walked out onto the veranda. The sun felt warm on his dark olive skin. He was now satisfied with his strategy, which would not only fulfill his desire for a challenge, but also present the possibility of increasing his control of the corporation where he was the CEO. He would soon be able to command the corporate board where Matthew was the chairman.

HE CALLED HIS SECRETARY, "LOUISE, PLEASE ARRANGE a meeting of our executive board. They have all worked very hard to make our corporation one of the most successful in the nation. I want to reward them with a working vacation, at my expense, on the island of St. Lucia. Since it is a working vacation, their wives will not be attending. I want their minds to concentrate only on business, not shopping trips to Castries."

"Sir," responded Louise, "are there other reasons for their wives not being invited? I mean, what do I say if they ask?"

Max frowned at Louise. "Just tell them it is a working vacation. I want time to get to know my executives better, especially the new vice presidents that have just been promoted. I never know when I will have to replace someone."

THE FLIGHT TO ST. LUCIA FROM NEW YORK WAS LONG. Max spent his time working on his computer. His first-class ticket provided the amenities that he required to be comfortable: the extra-wide seating, his favorite drinks and the never-ending desire of the flight attendants to please him. The plane landed at Hewanorra International Airport located near the town of Vieux Fort Quarter. It was a small, crowded airport but he passed through customs speedily. A shuttle to the lodge was already waiting for him on arrival. After a few courtesies, including a sweet tropical cocktail, he boarded the shuttle.

Max had arrived two days early in order to see that the arrangements for the meetings were complete. He wanted to ensure that the food and drinks were organized to his satisfaction. Max also wanted to conduct their sessions outdoors in the brilliant sun and cool tropical breezes.

THE MAIN REASON FOR HIS EARLY ARRIVAL, however, was to meet with a woman named Ladora Dubois. She ran a small novelty store just off the Soufriere main square. He entered the dark entrance of the shop and looked for Ladora, whom he had never met.

A small-framed woman with closely cut hair and long dangling mother-of-pearl earrings approached him. "Mr. Shell, Ladora has been waiting for you. She is upstairs. Please follow me."

Max followed the woman up the creaking stairs to a veranda that opened onto a view of the Gros Piton. On the other wall was a large floor-to-ceiling mirror that allowed the occupant of the veranda to see anyone climbing the stairs. Below were the rusty tin roofs of nearby houses and small businesses. The air was thick with the smell of tropical fruits. A sea breeze blew melodic wind chimes.

There seated at a small round green table was Ladora Dubois. Her skin was dark like the night sky. She wore her hair under a turban of greens, blues and reds. Her dress was wrapped about her tall, thin frame. At her feet was a large black mixed-breed dog that studied Max with an uncommon scrutiny.

Ladora motioned for Max to come closer and sit in front of her. Even though the table was round, she formed the head of the coarsely painted wood platform upon which were placed candles and small amulets. Tarot cards lay spread across the table. The Death card was predominantly displayed on top of the deck.

"As you know, my private investigator recommended your services," said Max, looking intently into her black recessed eyes. Eyes that were almost hidden from view by her prominent forehead. Max's attention was swiftly directed away from her to a movement in one corner of the room.

"Mr. Shell, do not bother yourself with shadows, it is only my pet python that has awakened from his lunch of mice. He will not bother you. You both share common tendencies."

Max did not know how to respond to her comment. For a moment, he was afraid that Fred Humphries had revealed too much about him to her. Then he realized that she, like all people, had a price for silence should the occasion arise.

"I am sure that Mr. Humphries explained everything to you. Where you able to find such a person?"

"There is no shortage of such women in St. Lucia, but only one can so completely entice a man she does not know. Her name is Anna D'Or."

"I like that name. *Anna of Gold*, a perfect name for such a person. Is she as beautiful as I hope she is? Can she be trusted to keep what I ask of her completely secret?"

"Yes, of course. She works for me. Should you ever see her on the streets of Castries or Soufriere, you will know that she is the one that we are now speaking of. No man who sees her can turn his face from her."

"I will pay you half of what is owed now and the other half when the entrapment has been completed." Max unsnapped the openings of his leather briefcase. He took out two sets of bills, giving her a glimpse of the rest. "I will leave you and your pet now," Max said without a smile. He turned and began to walk down the loose boards of the stairs. He looked at the mirror above him; there was no image to be seen of Ladora.

Surely, he thought, *she would have made a sound when she left the table.* Only the wind chime could be heard coming from the veranda.

THE FIVE TOP EXECUTIVES OF THE COMPANY ARRIVED as a group aboard a chartered jet. It too touched down at the nearby airport. A shuttle took them along the winding treacherous road that journeyed through the tropical rainforest that led to the lodge nestled high between the Pitons. Max walked out from the veranda of the lodge to greet them. "I hope you all arrived with your luggage." He paused. "I understand you had a brief wait in Atlanta, something to do with unauthorized luggage having been placed aboard. I don't object to delays when safety is involved." Max walked up to Matthew. "It is good to see you. How is Gina?"

"Doing well. I am sure that she will get together with the other wives and go shopping in Manhattan. I told her it was fine to spend money since she was not invited to St. Lucia. I imagine that the rest of them did the same. By the way, how is Margaret doing?"

"Great. I video chatted with her this morning. I think that she and Gina are planning some shopping trips together. I am afraid, however, that she is a little upset with me for not inviting the families down here, but I explained that this was only for top executives. A chance for us to work and relax at the same time. What man can relax if he is trying to please his wife?"

"A good point," replied Matthew.

"Let's have a drink once you get settled in," said Max. "I will meet you on the veranda."

MAX STOOD ON THE VERANDA looking at the warm blue Caribbean that lay far below the resort. He could see sailboats beating to windward as they chased the freshening wind. Large tropical clouds silently rode the wind above. Their tops painted by the sun and reflecting sea. Max felt once more in control. After a drink with Matthew, the meetings began in the open-air conference room. Max had prepared a PowerPoint designed to stimulate questions about the goals and objectives of their various divisions.

He had trays of hors d'oeuvres brought in for the meeting followed by pots of steaming hot coffee. He passed out the agenda for the daily sessions. The attendees were very pleased to see that only a few formal meetings were listed. The afternoons and evenings were completely free.

ON THE THIRD DAY OF THE MEETING, Max invited Matthew to join him for drinks at the bar. After a few rounds of rum and Coke, Max put his arm around his friend's shoulder. "Matthew, let's go into Sourfriere for some more exotic entertainment. I understand that there is a bar there that serves excellent Funky Monkeys."

"Well, why not?" said Matthew, trying not to slur his speech.

Max had the butler arrange for transportation to the cabaret Guillotine.

THE DRIVE TO SOUFRIERE STIRRED THE DRINKS within the stomachs of both men. The driver did not attempt to slow down on the hairpin curves that led across rapidly flowing streams and through the tropical rainforest. He used both lanes when making the curves, swerving back into the left lane only at the moment required to avoid a head-on collision with another vehicle.

Upon arrival, Matthew blinked his eyes as he got out of the taxi. He had expected to see an upscale bar, well-lit with diodes. Instead the Guillotine was dark around the entrance, illuminated by only a red neon light that blinked the name of the bar. Two locals sat on either side of the steps that led to the interior; their eyes followed the two men as they entered. Once inside, a young woman in a torn dress led them to a table next to a bamboo wall where a ceiling fan stirred the humid, warm air about them.

"What do you want to drink?" the hostess asked.

"Two Funky Monkeys on ice for a start," said Max.

Matthew looked at Max. "Are you sure about this place? This is definitely not what I expected. Good to know that you can come down a little every now and then."

"Relax. We are here to have fun. Of course, most of us have forgotten what that is like."

The hostess returned carrying a bamboo tray of Funky Monkeys.

Matthew looked at the drinks. "You must be counting on more fun than I am."

"Come on, Matthew. No need being a stick in the mud. Loosen up. Remember, you were the number one asshole in our NROTC class. You owe me one for taking my slot."

"Come on, Max. The number two spot is a position of honor. For active duty, we were both awarded career-enhancing billets. By the way, who is that beautiful woman lurking in the shadows?"

"Hell if I know," said Max, beckoning her to join them.

As she emerged from the shadows, her features appeared more

beautiful than either one of them had imagined.

Max leaned over and said in a pretended whisper, "Such beauty deserves a warm welcome."

D'Or sat down at the table. She moved her chair closer to Matthew. "How are you doing, rich American?" she said without the strong local accent, but just a hint of the melodic Creole French.

"May I call you My Beautiful One?" Max asked.

"No, but your quiet friend can," she replied, looking into Matthew's eyes as though probing for a weakness.

Max looked at her. "Well Matthew, it looks like you have won again."

TWO HOURS PASSED AND THEN THREE. Max waited for his friend in the now empty bar. The bartender had fallen asleep in a lounge chair next to the mahogany bar. Max's eyes felt heavy and soon he too was asleep. He was awakened by the sound of a crowing rooster that paraded upon the steps to the bar. Back and forth he walked crowing loudly. The smell of stale alcohol and cigarette smoke lingered in the bar as though waiting to escape through the open door that led into the street. Even though Max fell back asleep, he was soon awakened by the myriad sounds of voices coming from the street.

Then he heard someone walking down the stairs. It was Matthew. He was holding his head and walking with an unsteady gait.

"Good to see that you made it to morning with your pants still on. Tell me, is she as beautiful now as she was last night?"

Matthew slid into the chair next to Max. "I haven't felt like this since you and I pulled an overnighter in Naha. I am not sure what happened. I just remember smoking some pot with her, and then I don't remember what occurred next. I checked my wallet and my money is still there. I figured that she would have robbed me for everything I had. There must still be one virtuous hooker in the world."

Max felt his phone vibrating in his pocket. He took his Blackberry out and looked at the message. There was no message only a JPEG of Matthew naked, holding D'Or as she smiled.

"Shit. Matthew, what is this?" Max said, passing his Blackberry to Matthew.

"Oh no!" said Matthew.

"Well, my friend, it looks like your date took a selfie of you two."

"How did she know your cell phone number?" asked Matthew visibly shaken.

"It doesn't take a whiz kid to figure that one out. Obviously, she used the address book in your own phone. I wonder who else she sent the image to. The Board? Gina? Hell, she probably sent it to everyone in your directory."

"I will lose my position on the board as well as my wife if she did. Gina made it clear that she will leave me if I ever have an affair."

"Oh no. There are more photos of you two. Yep, I am afraid that she did send it to everyone in your address book. That includes the board, your wife and your friends," Max said in a concerned tone.

THAT EVENING MATTHEW LEFT THE RESORT and flew back to the States. Max felt confident that Gina would now be available for the asking. He knew that there was nothing like the vulnerability of an angry wife.

Having accomplished what he had set out to do, he arrived at the Hewanorra International Airport. He looked at the various shops and entered the Emerald Jewelry store. There he purchased a diamond and emerald necklace to give Gina. As the plane took off, he looked at the Pitons. Max felt a sadness that he could not explain. He felt the emptiness that a child feels when taken from its mother.

WHEN HE ARRIVED BACK IN NEW YORK, word was already spreading among the circle of top executives that dwelt there in their expensive suites. Their wives quickly spread the word about Matthew. It would only be a short time until one of the popular news magazines would publish censored images of Matthew's encounter – a few phone calls would see to that.

Three weeks later Matthew was asked to resign from the board. Two additional weeks passed before Max called Gina. She and Max spent many hours walking in Central Park and along the paths that followed the Hudson River. It was not long before Gina fell in love with Max.

In the early fall, they decided to watch the city on his yawl *Best Friends* while the evening turned into a misty night. As they cruised in the still warm air, they saw the lights of One World Trade Center reflecting upon the darkening waters of the bay.

"Gina, do you still miss Matthew?" asked Max.

"No, not so much. At first, I loved and hated him. A strange mixture of emotions. I could not forgive him for betraying me in such a public fashion. His actions were so cheap and sordid." She paused. "I am thankful to have your love."

"Gina, you must forgive me, but I do not love you."

Gina stared at him silently. He could see her tears reflecting the lights of the bridge that they had just passed under. "How can that be?" she asked.

"Matthew did not betray you. I did," he said loudly above the roar of the diesel that powered the large vessel.

"How can that be? You did nothing. None of us knew he was suicidal. I think he could not stand the scandal that followed. People can be very cruel," she said.

"He was a weak man. I should never have invited him to St. Lucia," said Max.

"But why don't you love me?" she pleaded, striking his chest softly in exaggerated blows.

"You see, I feel too guilty for loving my best friend's wife. When I am with you, I sense his presence. That is all I can and will say."

THAT NIGHT HE DREAMED OF THE PITONS AND HIS FRIEND. In his dream, a hurricane was approaching the island. He reached for someone's hand but could not grasp it. Then the dream ended and he was alone in his suite that overlooked Central Park.

CHAPTER THIRTEEN
Garden of Eden

A Viper Sleeps

Refuge sought within the warm tropic night.
The Pitons rise above the swell to beckon the dream.
Does love flourish or is it silenced by the heart?

Within the Garden of Eden it waits.
Under the breadfruit tree, coiled, the viper sleeps.
Awakened by the scent of flesh, it strikes unseen.

LINERS WITH EXPECTANT TOURISTS ARRIVE DAILY. The ships arrive two at a time and leave in a single-file convoy by evening light. The bars are the cathedrals of the docks. The holy candles, the small lamps that line the walls among the illuminated ads for drinks. The confessions received by the bartenders. They listen and do not speak.

Don't tourists realize that there are no answers here? The voice of reality does not speak in a tropic port. Eyes are closed to the vessels rusting at the entryway to the port. Indifferent officials stamp the passports as the sweet smell of tropical fruit sits in the warehouses about the piers.

With the sound of backing horn, the large steamers leave the docks casting off their lines. A few stragglers remain lost on shore, those that lounge and fall asleep in the steamy baths of volcanic mud.

The steamer's lights glow like a Los Vegas night in the desert of the sea. Soon they turn towards the islands to the south – Barbados, Tobago and Trinidad –or to the north – St. Martin, Martinique and the Virgins.

Tourists come expecting everything but what they find. Straw markets, solicitors of beads and the bars that line the quays. The tropical odors of jasmine, scarlet chenille and wild orchids greet them intertwined with scents of rum, gin and vodka.

There is a strange light that covers the mountains of Saint Lucia. It is unlike any other color that Max had ever seen. It is a soft orange yellow light not related to any weather phenomena seen in less tropic lands.

Coconut trees and banana plants fight for their existence in the valleys formed by the steep mountains. The people are filled with laughter and broad smiles, yet expressions change as the tourists arrive. Goats stand in the house and watch the American, Brits and Canadians ride by.

Cruise ships from around the world enter the main port city.

At night, they appear like floating Christmas trees strung with myriad white lights. They debark their passengers who roam the various markets of the port city. A cargo ship rides at anchor just beyond the stark brown cliffs that fall precipitously into the Caribbean.

Away from Castries, the waves hit the cliffs and rebound into the sea. At night the frogs and crickets sound as well as the birds that sing in darkness. An annoying popping sound from brown-spotted frogs is heard above all others.

Tropical sunsets in a myriad number of colors precede the night. The sun falls into the warm multicolored sea. The hot humid seas off the coast of Africa cast their hurricanes toward St. Lucia like bowling balls hurled towards the pins of islands. They knock down the houses and trees in their mad rush towards the Gulf of Mexico.

The voices of the people, like the swells of the sea, rise and fall in varied tones.

MAX LURED MARGARET INTO VISITING ST. LUCIA. He had been captivated by the beauty and exotic nature of the island on his previous visit. After his plan to betray his friend had worked, he felt that the island was a more than inviting destination, a place of victory. He and Margaret planned on staying a few days at Deux Amis in order to enjoy the New Year's festivities. At the conclusion of their stay, their already leased villa would be ready for an extended vacation.

Their cottage faced the crescent-shaped Brune de Montagnes beach. Located high above the cliff, it was surrounded by coconut and flowering trees. It was well-guarded, private and inaccessible to others.

WARM RAIN FELL UPON THE ISLAND LIKE AN APOLOGY from a

recent and unexpected storm. Pauline and Sidney sat across from Max and Margaret. Reluctant friends made on the van ride from the airport. It was Pauline's second marriage as well as Sidney's. His wife had died of lung cancer earlier. Pauline was larger than life. Full of energy and a chance taker. Sidney needed to prove that he too could take chances. He had always dreamed of snorkeling beneath the Pitons, those tall solitary cones of ancient volcanoes that gave fiery birth to the island long before the Arawak Indians arrived and later, the conflicts between the English and French. The Pitons stood like centennials of creation.

After the meal, Max indicated to Margaret and their new friends that he was very tired from the trip and needed to retire for the afternoon.

On the way to their room, Margaret asked, "Was Pauline not good-looking enough to make you want to talk with her more? You were very dismissive back there."

Max looked at her. "It is always best to be honest with strangers or they will become unwanted friends. Brune de Montagnes is too small to have unanticipated friends."

Quickly they arrived at their butler's suite room with its beautiful heavy mahogany furniture and dark wood trim. Their view looked out over the Caribbean Sea, high above the waves that pounded upon the decaying volcanic rock below. Each moment the sea changed, each moment the light altered all that it touched including the emotions of the guests.

As they sat making casual conversation, the ocean's incessant roar joined the table. Beyond them in the island sun was a striking tree with a deathlike stance and red blooms defying nature and man. Its leafless branches carried a solitary crown of red flowers.

In the bright sun, the old sat isolated from the hard bodies of the young. Their stares were concealed by dark sunglasses – not stares of sexual awareness, but hidden longings concealed within loose muscles, sagging breasts and stomachs.

The Brune de Montagnes at first bothered him. An older man among a crowd of firm bodies. Women in bikinis and men with arms tattooed like the natives of the Amazon basin. He realized that age isolated him from others.

At first, his wife did not acknowledge such a feeling, but he knew that she sensed it, too. While drinking coffee on the open veranda, Margaret related what was all too apparent to him, "You know, a young couple was surprised when I told them that I still rooted for my university's football team. They did not realize that we do not change inside. Age is irrelevant to emotion."

Stray cats sat upon the porch, patient, waiting and undisturbed by the loud blast of a ship's horn that sounded the departure of yet another vessel. Tourists sat together drinking unlimited amounts of liquor, masks made of piña colada and Piton beer. A Disney world of poverty and overt desire.

In the late evening of their arrival, Max and Margaret awoke in their beach chairs to the pounding of the sea, sunburned where the myriad lotions had not protected their bodies. That evening the New Year's Eve party promised to be all that they had hoped it would be. It was the festivities of the evening that had first attracted Max's attention to his computer screen while searching the site for a winter vacation. Perhaps even more important to his choice was the deep longing that he had to return to St. Lucia, a strong feeling of anticipation for that not consciously known. Perhaps it was the recurring dreams that led him back as well.

MAX'S CASUAL FLIRTATIONS AT THE BEACH only yielded new frustrations. That evening Brune de Montagnes prepared a magnificent New Year's dinner and celebration. They quickly found a table away from the serving line and closest to the illuminated swimming pool. Next to Max was Mark, a friendly owner of Italian restaurants. Mark had started his businesses in Cancun and Canada. Next to him was the beautiful Julie. A striking young woman of twenty-four whom he identified as his personal trainer. He said that they had known each other for five years.

Max asked, "Are you two engaged?"

"No," replied Mark, "no point in breaking the charm."

On the other side of Max's wife sat Frank and Erica. He was thirty-two and she was twenty-six. They were on a two-week honeymoon and very much in love.

Celebratory cheers sounded as fireworks exploded in showers of colors far above the beach. The year had not been his best one. He was well aware that time was passing far too quickly. He acknowledged the pain in his hip and now a headache from too many coconut drinks filled with milk and rum.

THERE WERE NO SOUNDS, NO VEHICLES TRAVELING in the new morning dawn. The soft sound of a radio played West Indies music. Not too loud, but like remnants of the Caribbean night. He felt safe in the carefully controlled atmosphere of the resort and the embracing arms that only money can buy. The security was no more real that the simulated affection in his marriage.

The day arrived with the call of the blackbirds. The night frogs ceased their conversations. That afternoon they left for Soufriere, a small town flushed with poverty. The Creole language sounded with the melodious quality of tropical birds. Just as before, men sat staring towards the street. Women carried on conversations as they walked about with laundry on their heads. Sunburned tourists debarked from catamarans.

The streets of Soufriere did not seem safe as those of the resort. It conveyed a mixture of both monetary need and dislike fostered by those who came to the town to spend money, drink rum and leave. The local hospital seemed more like a waiting room than a clinic. There was no apparent medical assistance, only the appearance that there might be. HIV had struck the small town hard. Neither the tropical mountains, the multicolored sea nor the intoxicating drinks condoned caution.

As Max looked at the men walking slowly along the road, he noticed that several gripped cutlasses, their long blades reflecting the glare of the sun.

"Why are the men carrying such long knives?" he asked the chauffeur.

"Mon, they are used to cut the coconuts open. No need for you to worry, you are not edible," Aden said, laughing. "You only need to worry if they get mad at you. Look at their grip. If it tightens, offer them a Piton."

"What do you mean? I thought that was the name of the two-boob mountains," joked Margaret. It was apparent that Max resented his wife's friendliness towards the hired driver.

"Yes, that is correct, but it is also the name of our island beer."

"Oh, I see. Hell, I will buy him a six pack if that is what Tonto wants," joked Max.

"Tonto? What do you mean?"

"It is just a term I use when I don't know a person's name," Max said somewhat nervously. He remembered that he was in their country, not his own.

Max looked at the small village from the safety of his automobile. The houses and shops were very small with dim-lit interiors. Some of the houses sat at various angles, products of poverty and neglect. Their sole purpose was shelter from the frequent showers of the tropical island.

The driver continued to honk his horn.

"You seem to be honking incessantly," said Max in a voice that conveyed his agitation.

"Mon, I just talking with the horn," the driver replied. "You not used to St. Lucia. You honk to everyone you know or who smiles at you. If you don't honk, people think you are ignoring them. It is part of the island sounds, just like the crows and frogs."

"Okay. Ever since I arrived here, nothing seems to make sense. For example, you are driving way too fast on the left side of the road. What if there is a mudslide? Also, I can't believe that when we stopped at a tourist attraction so I can go to the restroom, I found a state hostess feeding her neighbor's chickens in the exhibit hall."

"Rich Americans always uptight. You don't understand."

"My God, how do people eat here? No one seems to be working."

"No problem. We all grow our own food in the yard. If you like mangoes, you plant a mango tree. If you like bananas, you have banana trees. No one hungry if living in a family village. Everyone fed."

"Yah, but how can anyone afford a place to live? I see one-room shacks overlooking a million-dollar view. This place is ripe for development."

"We don't want your development, not good for nature. No problem for people to have land, we build on family land. We share our property. In family villages, everyone is related. Here people live a long time so our grandmothers know where the property lines are if anyone bothers to ask."

"That would never work in the States. We really don't trust one another, especially relatives. If you want to make a bad loan, call a cousin."

"Sad, Mon."

"The richer a person becomes, the more greedy the bastard becomes," said Max as he looked out the car window towards the mountains with their mixture of exotic plants. Tall coconut trees clung to almost vertical mountain slopes that led to streams that rapidly flowed into the villages below and then into the sea.

The car left the small town of Soufriere and climbed rapidly through the rainforest towards the villa. Max ignored the waves of the bead sellers, sensing their inner hostility. The car sped past coconut palms, invasive bamboos, ferns and wild orchids.

He noticed a young woman holding a snake around her neck as the car slowed. She pressed the mouth of the python with her fingers to keep it from biting her. "What is she, a snake charmer?" said Max in a sarcastic tone.

"No, Manuela is trying to earn money. Her brothers catch the snake for her. She had a really big one named Patrick but he died. Her new snake does not earn her enough money. Tourists like big snakes."

THE DRIVER SLOWED DOWN. "Do you want to have your picture taken with the python? She only accepts donations."

"Donations?" asked Max. When the driver did not reply, he said, "No, don't stop, but she looks so young. She is really pretty. Why doesn't she move to Castries and try to make a real living?"

"What for? Her family will provide for her and her brothers protect her. No one would look out for Manuela in Castries."

"On your way back to Soufriere, tell her that I will find a place for her to work at the villa. If her attitude is good and she is smart enough, my wife and I can use her during our three months here. It will pay more than wrapping a python around the neck of a tourist. The owner of the estate said that he was currently understaffed. It would feel good to help someone... you know what I mean."

"Yes, mon, I know what you mean. I will talk to her grandmother."

ON THE VERANDA OF THE GREAT HOUSE, the smell of approaching rain came before the drops arrived. Wind and rain brought the odors of the tropical rainforest to the villa. The rain was expected and fell gently at first upon the broad leaves of the forest ferns and sluiced quickly down the tips of the palm fronds. Only the brief showers sustained the rainforest and every living thing in it – whether insect, beast or man.

Fast, brief showers fell from the sky, yet when Max searched for clouds, there were none present. Magical rains of softness scented the air. Then suddenly they stopped, reflections of the sun appeared on the damp leaves and rivulets of light.

IN THE TWILIGHT, THE STARK GRANDEUR OF THE PITONS appeared as if they were columns supporting the blue sky above them. The breasts of St. Lucia, the natives called them. They are a symbol of the island that fed the imagination of the tourists. The pungent smell of boiling sulfa infiltrated the vents of the chauffeur-driven car. The mountain above denuded by the breath of the twelve-kilometer caldera.

CHAPTER FOURTEEN
Manuela

MAX WAS NOT CERTAIN WHY HE HAD BEEN SO BOLD as to hire Manuela after seeing her holding the python on the winding road that connected the villa to Castries. Perhaps it was the intense expression in her eyes that so fascinated him. She had stood like a subject in a Paul Gauguin painting surrounded by the wild flowering vines of the nearby jungle.

Approaching the villa, Margaret asked, "You can't be serious about hiring a stranger, surely not. You have not done a background check. Besides, she could be a thief."

"How can you judge her when you know absolutely nothing about her?" asked Max.

"And I suppose you do?"

Max did not reply as they neared the metal gates that led to the estate.

AFTER UNPACKING, THEY WALKED TO THE VERANDA for dinner – a meal of fresh lobsters in excellent French sauce. Steamed asparagus sat next to the French bread and olive oil accompanied by a fine white wine chilled in a silver holder.

Max looked at the multicolored light that fell upon the Pitons. He looked towards Margaret. "Just about perfect."

"Max, what would make it completely perfect?"

He did not answer but instead dipped his lobster in the sauce, then tasted the wine, his eyes never leaving the crest of the sea. The staff stood nearby in their service uniforms, wearing customary spotless white gloves.

"You know, Max, what would make it perfect to me would be if love were present," she said without looking at him.

His voice only replied to her in silent words.

Max looked towards Melon, his server. "Did you ever contact Manuela's grandmother to see if she is available?"

"Yes, sir. In fact, she is standing there in the shadow of the banyan to ask you for permission to serve."

Max looked in the direction of the large tree that reminded him so much of India. There in its shadows stood a long figure. Max motioned for her to approach. She proceeded to walk slowly in his direction.

"Sir, I am the woman with the python. May I wait upon you and the madam?"

Max smiled. "Come on now, Manuela. Be bold! Of course, you can serve us. In fact, you can bring us more wine to enjoy. Melon will show you were it is located."

Margaret looked sternly at Max. "Do you know what you are doing? How do you know if she understands anything about serving? She could embarrass us in front of guests." After a pause, she continued, "I still don't trust these island natives. They seem like they are hiding something. I know it is just a feeling. We should have hired a server through an employment agency. God only knows how many lawyers you own. Why not have one of them check her out before offering the goddam keys to the house?"

Even Max was shocked at the tone of her voice: knowing, accusing, and condemning in tone.

"Are you planning on having sex with her later?" asked Margaret.

"Get ahold of yourself before we are asked to leave the island. Do you think that all I live for is to have an affair? If anyone really gets to know you, I will be found faultless regardless of what I choose to do in my personal life."

"You bastard!" Margaret said, pushing her chair back from the table. Melon struggled to keep her from falling as the corner of her chair caught on a small protruding stone embedded in the floral design of the tile floor.

IN THE HEAT OF THE AFTERNOONS, Max made it a habit to sit on the veranda where Manuela served him alone. They did not talk but instead communicated through expressions, perhaps a smile, a nod. To a casual observer, their language might appear childlike, almost primitive when first observed. For Max, it was wonderful not to choose words to express emotions.

Gradually, his eyes memorized the contours of her face. His gaze traveled to her body yet they did not touch nor did they often speak. They communicated like images on an impressionist's canvas.

Occasionally Margaret would join him for a drink. Yet in her presence, he continued to study Manuela as a patron of the arts would a desired painting he wanted to acquire. Should someone ask him what was behind the attraction, he could not have explained it.

Max remembered looking at a Van Gogh in the Musée d'Orsay in Paris. The colors were more than lifelike, the brilliance of visual emotion expressed through hue and texture. He stood before it entranced by its beauty. Day after day, he returned to the museum only to look upon this one painting until forced to leave by an attendant.

As THE SUN RESTED UPON THE WAVES OF THE SEA, Manuela approached him, placing her hand upon his. "Come with me tonight. We go to the Pitons," she said in a barely audible whisper.

"Why would I do that? Mosquitoes and slippery rocks? No, thank you. I had much rather read," Max said looking into her dark, black eyes.

Her eyes returned his gaze alluringly. A sense of desire arose uncontrollably within him. "It is the festival of the Black Moon," she whispered.

"What are you talking about?" asked Max.

"The first full moon in August is referred to as the Black Moon. Many bad things happened on that night long ago. My people prayed to the moon to stop the curse. Even though no bad things now happen, it is still referred to as the Black Moon. The goddess has blessed us."

"I thought that the majority of your people on St. Lucia are Catholic," said Max. "Why are they worshipping a pagan symbol?"

"We worship what is real to us. The British and Americans have never taken the time to understand the people of St. Lucia."

"Well, let me apologize to you for the slavery," he said sarcastically.

"You mock me."

"No, Manuela, I am praising you. Innocence is something that we Westerners no longer have. Believe what you will. It does not matter. I will accept your invitation. Perhaps I will learn something." He looked towards the sea. "May your goddess protect us from ourselves."

He was now more willing to take risks in his unhappiness than before. Max knew not what to expect on the mountain, but that no longer mattered. There would not be any hidden agendas awaiting him, nothing that he could not face and overcome.

AFTER MARGARET HAD GONE TO SLEEP on the third floor of the villa, Max rose from his bed. He had not slept but only stared at the Gros Piton while lying on his side. He watched the arrival of the mist as it began to cover the steep sides of the mountain. Gros Piton was soon adorned in the garment of the sea. Suddenly, moonlight arrived upon its surface after breaking through the dark clouds that nourished the nearby rainforest. In his room, he heard a mosquito humming but paid no attention to it as he dressed.

MAX HAD DELIBERATELY PARKED THE RANGE ROVER at the entrance to the estate so that Margaret would not hear him crank the automobile. He saw Manuela waiting next to the car. Her skin, hair and eyes were adorned in moonlight. Wrapped about her was a sarong whose true colors could not be seen in the moonlight. Max quickly entered the car without saying a word.

ONCE CLEAR OF THE GATES, MANUELA SAT QUIETLY as Max drove in fitful bursts of speed along the mountainous curves.

"You mentioned arranging for a discreet person to meet us in Soufriere. I assume that he is a guide or something like that." Max paused. "Who is he?"

"He is my spiritual advisor," she replied.

"Are you taking me to a Seventh-day Adventist service?" Max said with a degree of mockery in his voice.

"It is a religious service, but not one sponsored by the Seventh-day Adventist."

"Catholic?" he questioned.

"Yes and no. There are many faiths on the island," she replied.

THEY DROVE THROUGH THE DARKENED VILLAGE OF SOUFRIERE. Loud music no longer danced through the streets. No nude child directed traffic. Only a few bars remained open, their entryways concealed by hanging cloths and bamboo curtains. Even in the darkness of the streets, he could feel the stares of the prostitutes that waited at the mouth of their dens while others slept within.

Moonlight reflected off the tin roofs and the Caribbean Sea. Inside the small wood huts, oil lamps could be seen burning.

"Manuela, Soufriere is a different city at night. The moonlight conceals so much."

"Yes, the full moon changes everything, even us," she replied in perfect English. Yet the melodic quality of her native accent was still present.

"I can't believe how beautiful the ocean has become," Max said quietly as though speaking to himself. "Even more beautiful that the many hues I see from the villa – all shades of greens, blues and yellows… and yet it is only moonlight."

After meeting a man in Soufriere in silence, Max and Manuela changed positions in the automobile. The unknown man quickly drove past the dormant volcano with its oozing sulfuric odor. Into the night they hurried past the silhouettes of bamboo and coconut palms.

CLOSE TO THE BASE OF THE GROS PITON, they ascended a narrow road, almost a trail, into the rainforest filled with the noises of a tropical night. Soon the sound of a waterfall was heard. Nearby, steam rose from the pits of boiling mud. The Land Rover captured and retained the volcanic scent as it bounced on the rocky streambeds.

Because of their isolation and the lack of conversation, Max began to get nervous. "I must ask you, where are you taking me and why?"

Manuela replied, "You have been very kind to me. No other man from a foreign land has seen what you will tonight. You will feel what no other man has felt."

THE CAR STOPPED ABRUPTLY, and the silent driver opened Manuela's door. He then, much to Max's surprise, bowed slightly before her. Around them were flaming lanterns; the scent of burning kerosene was carried by the gentle land breeze.

"Manuela, what is this place? I hear the sound of a waterfall."

"Max, I have taken you to my church. You need to relax and feel the peace and energy around you," she said, handing him a drink in a pewter mug.

The liquid tasted warm like the juice of a freshly cut coconut. He wanted very much to please her. The taste was bittersweet. Immediately the sound of drums and metal instruments were heard. Manuela began to sway with the beat of the wind, sea and waterfall. A nearby night fowl announced its presence with deep long calls adding to the symphony of the night.

Despite his conservative nature, Max felt his own body swaying with that of hers. As they danced, she began to remove her sarong. The tempo of the music increased as did the passion that was now aroused within him.

Manuela laughed at the manifestation of his desire. Soon their wet bodies were enjoined as was the music to the night. They were suspended in the warm muddy water heated by the center of the earth. Clouds of steam rose about them as he penetrated her, both of them engulfed in nocturnal passion.

CHAPTER FIFTEEN
Heat of the Sun

THE HEAT OF THE SUN AWAKENED MAX. The hard volcanic rock on which his head rested magnified his discomfort. Rising steam and the dense jungle of the Pitons surrounded him. A heavy rain was falling, creating rivulets of water about his body. The water fell from his naked shoulders. There were no signs that anything other than the natural rhythms of the night had ever occurred in the isolated heart of the jungle.

His clothes lay scattered about the boulders that lined the cascading stream of clear cold currents that mixed with the steamy muddy waters of the cauldron.

HE STAGGERED DOWN A SELDOM-USED JUNGLE PATH and managed to catch a ride with a local grower. After a generous tip, he was taken to the gates of his own villa. It occurred to him that Manuela had already taken the Land Rover back. Max planned on venting his anger once the two of them were alone.

He managed to enter his own bedroom without disturbing Margaret. There he quickly showered and dressed in fresh clothing.

Max shouted down the hall, "Margaret, I feel very depressed this morning. I think I will walk along the beach before the wind becomes too strong. I know it is raining, but the air is warm."

Margaret answered, "Max, just remember that in a few hours a hurricane will arrive. I think that it is best that you stay and prepare the villa for its arrival. While it is predicted to be no more than a Category 1 storm, it can increase rapidly in strength."

"No, I will be gone only a short time. Melon can prepare everything. Just tell him to take the furniture off the veranda and to close all of the shutters."

She did not see him as he left the estate and descended the narrow steep path that led to the sea below.

WHEN TWO HOURS HAD PASSED, SHE CALLED CHRIS CASEY. Chris had moved to the island two years ago and had built a large house overlooking Soufriere and the dark sand below it. She knew that Chris often used his telescope to see anyone walking along the beach since the entryway path to his house could be reached from the shoreline.

"I am a little bit concerned about Max," said Margaret over the static-filled phone. "He said that he wanted to walk along the beach to look at the large breakers preceding the storm. Did you happen to see him?"

"I saw two people on the beach this morning readying a small skiff. I am sure that one of them was Max and the other person a dark woman, perhaps from India. At that distance, I cannot be sure."

"You mean dark like Manuela?"

"Yes, perhaps. I waved at them from my balcony, but they did not acknowledge my presence. The odd thing about it was that Max appeared so much younger than he is. He moved like someone in his early twenties. The woman also looked very young. Like I said, she was very dark in complexion. I cannot imagine why they would be launching a skiff knowing that a hurricane is approaching St. Lucia." Chris continued, "When I last saw them, they were raising what appeared to be a lateen sail like you would expect to see on an Arab dhow... you know, one of those vessels that you can find sailing the coast of Seychelles. Then my phone rang. It was the island police telling me to ensure that my house was well-boarded. The storm was approaching faster than predicted.

"When I looked back on the beach, I could not see them or the skiff any more, just large waves crashing upon the shore of the Gros Piton. If it had been Max – and I can't be completely sure – he was always a survivalist, perhaps he is safe now in some remote harbor."

"Perhaps, perhaps," Margaret replied, looking at the spume-strewn waters of the Caribbean Sea.

About the Author

Franklin Lafayette King was born in the Panhandle of Texas and spent much of his youth on the Blackland Prairie. He received a commission through the University of Texas in Austin and soon became involved in the Vietnam Conflict. After additional academic preparation, he moved to the foothills of the Appalachians. In addition to combat, he experienced both the eyes of a hurricane and an F-4 tornado, events that were to influence much of his later work.

www.ingramcontent.com/pod-product-compliance
Lightning Source LLC
Chambersburg PA
CBHW050525260626
47157CB00004B/1476